Laura E. H. Richards

Toto's Merry Winter

Laura E. H. Richards

Toto's Merry Winter

ISBN/EAN: 9783337255657

Printed in Europe, USA, Canada, Australia, Japan

Cover: Foto ©Andreas Hilbeck / pixelio.de

More available books at **www.hansebooks.com**

TOTO'S MERRY WINTER.

BY

LAURA E. RICHARDS,

AUTHOR OF

"THE JOYOUS STORY OF TOTO," "FIVE MICE IN A MOUSETRAP,"
"SKETCHES AND SCRAPS," ETC., ETC.

BOSTON:
ROBERTS BROTHERS.
1887.

TO

The Blind Children of the Perkins Institution,

WHO HAVE LISTENED TO THE FIRST

"STORY OF TOTO,"

THIS SECOND AND LAST PART OF HIS ADVENTURES

IS AFFECTIONATELY DEDICATED.

TOTO'S MERRY WINTER.

CHAPTER I.

IT was evening, — a good, old-fashioned winter evening, cold without, warm and merry within. The snow was falling lightly, softly, with no gusts of wind to trouble it and send it whirling and drifting hither and thither. It covered the roof with a smooth white counterpane, tucking it in neatly and carefully round the edges; it put a tall conical cap on top of the pump, and laid an ermine fold over his long and impressive nose. Myriads of curious little flakes pattered softly — oh! very softly — against the windows of the cottage, pressing against the glass to see what was going on inside, and saying, "Let us in! let us in! please do!" But nobody seemed inclined to let them in, so they were forced to content themselves with looking.

Indeed, the aspect of the kitchen was very inviting, and it is no wonder that the little cold flakes wanted to get in. A great fire was crackling and leaping on the hearth. The whole room seemed to glow and glitter: brass saucepans, tin platters, glass window-panes, all cast their very brightest glances toward the fire, to show him that they appreciated his efforts. Over this famous fire, in the very midst of the dancing, flickering tongues of yellow flame, hung a great black soup-kettle, which was almost boiling over with a sense of its own importance, and a kindly consciousness of the good things cooking inside it.

"Bubble! b-r-r-r-r! bubble! hubble!" said the black kettle, with a fat and spluttering enunciation.

> "Bubble, hubble! b-r-r-r-r-r-r! bubble!
> Lots of fun, and very little trouble!"

On the hob beside the fire sat the tea-kettle, a brilliant contrast to its sooty neighbor. It was of copper, so brightly burnished that it shone like the good red gold. The tea-kettle did not bubble, — it considered bubbling rather vulgar; but it was singing very merrily, in a clear pleasant voice, and pouring out volumes of steam from its slender copper nose. "I am doing all I can to make myself agrecable!" the tea-kettle said to itself. "I am boiling just right, — hard enough to make a good cheerful noise, and not so hard as to boil all the water away. And *why* that beast should sit and glower at me there as he is doing, is more than I can understand."

"That beast" was a raccoon. I think some of you children may have seen him before. He was sitting in front of the fire, with his beautiful tail curled comfortably about his toes; and he certainly *was* staring very hard at the tea-kettle. Presently the kettle, in pure playfulness and good-will, lifted its cover a little and let out an extra puff of snowy steam; and at that the raccoon gave a jump, and moved farther away from the fire, without ever taking his eyes off the kettle.

The fact is, that for the first time in his life the raccoon knew what *fear* was. He was afraid — mortally afraid — of that tea-kettle.

"Don't tell me!" he had said to Toto, only the day before, "don't tell *me* it is n't alive! It breathes, and it talks, and it moves, and if that isn't being alive I don't know what is."

"Coon, how utterly absurd you are!" cried Toto, laughing. "It *does n't* move, except when some one takes it up, of course, or tilts it on the hob."

"Toto," said the raccoon, speaking slowly and impressively, "as sure as you are a living boy, I saw that kettle take off the top of its head and look out of its own inside, only last night. And before that," he added, looking rather shamefaced, "I — I just put my paw in to see what there was inside, and the creature caught it and took all the skin off."

But here Toto burst into a fit of laughter, and said, "Served you right!" which was so rude that the raccoon went off and sat under the table, in a huff.

So this time, when the kettle took off the top of its head, Coon did not run out into the shed, as he had done before, because he was ashamed when he remembered Toto's laughter. He only moved away a little, and looked and felt thoroughly uncomfortable.

But now steps were heard outside. The latch clicked, the door opened, and Toto and Bruin entered, each carrying a foaming pail of milk. They brushed the snow from their coats, and Toto took off his, which the good bear could not well do; then, when they had carried their milk-pails into the dairy, they came and sat down by the fire, with an air of being ready to enjoy themselves. The raccoon winked at them by way of greeting, but did not speak.

"Well, Coon," said Bruin, in his deep bass voice, "what have you been doing all the afternoon? Putting your tail in curl-papers, eh?"

"Not at all," replied the raccoon with dignity, "I have been sweeping the hearth; sweeping it," he added, with a majestic curl of his tail, "in a manner which *some* people [here he glanced superciliously at the bear] could hardly manage."

"I am sure," said the boy Toto, holding out his hands toward the ruddy fire-blaze, "it is a blessing that Bruin has no tail. Just fancy how he would go knocking things about! Why, it would be two yards long, if it were in the same proportion as yours, Coon!"

"Hah!" said the raccoon, yawning, "very likely. And what have you two been doing, pray, since dinner?"

"I have been splitting kindling-wood," said Toto, "and building a snow fort, and snowballing Bruin. And he has—"

"I have been talking to the pig," said Bruin, very gravely. "The pig. Yes. He is a very singular animal, that pig. Is it true," he added, turning to Toto, "that he has never left that place, that sty, since he was born?"

"Never, except to go into the yard by the cow-shed," said Toto. "His sty opens into the yard, you know. But I don't think he cares to go out often."

"That is what he said," rejoined the bear. "That is what struck me as so very strange. He said he never went out, from one winter to another. And when I asked why, he snorted, and said, 'For fear the wind should blow my bristles off.' Said it in a very rude way, you know. I don't think his manners are good. I shall not go to see him again, except in the way of taking his food to him. But here we sit, talking," continued the bear, rising, "when we ought to be getting supper. Come! come! you lazy fellows, and help me set the table."

With this, the good bear proceeded to tie a huge white apron round his great black, shaggy body, and began to poke the fire, and to stir the contents of the soup-kettle with a long wooden spoon, — all with a very knowing air, as if he had done nothing but cook all his life. Meanwhile, the raccoon and Toto spread a clean cloth on the table, and set out cups and plates, a huge brown bowl for the bear, a smaller one for the raccoon, etc. Bread and milk, and honey and baked apples came next; the soup-kettle yielded up a most savory stew, made of everything good, and onions besides; and finally, when all was ready, Toto ran and knocked at the door of his grandmother's room, crying, "Granny, dear! supper is ready, and we are only waiting for you."

The door opened, and the blind grandmother came out, with the little squirrel perched on her shoulder.

"Good evening to you all!" she said, with her sweet smile and her pretty little old-fashioned courtesy. "We have been taking a nap, Cracker and I, and we feel quite refreshed and ready for the evening."

The grandmother looked ten years younger, Toto was constantly telling her, than she did the year before; and, indeed, it was many years since she had had such a pleasant, easy life. Helpful as Toto had always been to

her, still, he was only a little boy, though a
very good one ; and by far the larger share
of work had fallen to the old lady herself.
But now there were willing hands — paws,
I should say — to help her at every turn.
The bear washed and cooked, churned and
scrubbed, with never-tiring energy and good-
will. The raccoon worked very hard indeed :
he said so, and nobody took the trouble to
contradict him. He swept the kitchen occasionally, and did a good deal of graceful and
genteel dusting with his long bushy tail, and
tasted all the food that Bruin cooked, to see
if it had the proper flavor. Besides these
heavy duties, he caught rats, teased the cow,
pulled the parrot's tail whenever he got a
chance, and, as he expressed it, "tried to
make things pleasant generally." The little
squirrel had constituted himself a special attendant on "Madam," as the forest-friends
all called the grandmother. He picked up
her ball of yarn when it rolled off her lap,
as it was constantly doing. He cracked nuts
for her, brought her the spices and things

when she made her famous gingerbread, and
went to sleep in her ample pocket when he
had nothing else to do. As for the wood-
pigeon and the parrot, they were happy and
contented, each in her own way, each on her
own comfortable perch, at her own window.

Thus had all Toto's summer playmates become winter friends, fast and true; and it
would be difficult to find a happier party
than that which gathered round the bright
fire, on this and every other evening, when
the tea-things were put away, the hearth
newly swept, and a great tin-pan full of nuts
and apples placed on the clean hearth-stone.
Only one of the animals whom you remember in Toto's summer story was missing from
the circle; that was the woodchuck. But he
was not very far off. If you had looked into
a certain little cupboard near the fireplace,—
a quaint little cupboard, in which lived three
blue ginger-jars and a great pewter tankard,
— you would have seen, lying in the warmest
corner, next the fireplace, something which
looked at first sight like a large knitted ball

of red yarn. On looking closer, you would have seen that it was a ball of brown fur, enclosed in a knitted covering. If you had taken off the covering and unrolled the ball, you would have found that it was a woodchuck, sound asleep.

Poor Chucky had found it quite impossible to accept the new arrangement. He had always been in the habit of sleeping all through the winter; and while the other animals had succeeded, after a long time, in conquering their sleepiness (though it was still a very common thing to find Bruin asleep over the churn, and Coon had a way of creeping 'into Toto's bed at odd times during the day), the woodchuck had succumbed entirely after the first week, and had now been asleep for a couple of months. At first, after he had dropped into his long slumber, the bear and the raccoon had played ball with him a good deal, tossing him about with great agility. But one day the living ball had fallen into the soup-kettle, where the water was so hot as to elicit a miserable

sleepy squeak from the victim, and the grandmother had promptly forbidden the game.
It was then that she knit the red-worsted
cover for poor Chucky, for she said she could
not bear to think of his sleeping all winter
with nothing over him; and she put him
away in the cupboard by the fireplace, and
wished him pleasant dreams as she closed
the door. So there the woodchuck lay, warm
and comfortable, but too sound asleep to
know anything about it. And the three
blue ginger-jars and the pewter tankard kept
watch over him, though they had their own
ideas about this stranger having been popped
in among them without so much as saying,
"By your leave!"

As I was saying, it was a happy party
that sat around the blazing fire. The grandmother in her high-backed armchair, knitting in hand; Toto sitting Turk-fashion on
the hearth-rug, his curly head resting on
the shaggy coat of the bear, who sat solemnly on his haunches, blinking with sober
pleasure at the fire; the raccoon on a low

hassock, which was his favorite seat in the evening, as it showed off his tail to great advantage; the parrot and the wood-pigeon perched on the high chair-back, and standing on one leg or two, as they felt inclined.

"Ah!" exclaimed the little squirrel, who had stationed himself on the top of Bruin's head, as a convenient and suitable place, "Ah! now this is what *I* call comfort. Snowing fast outside, is n't it, Bruin?"

"Yes!" replied the bear.

"That makes it all the more jolly inside!" said the squirrel. "What are we to do this evening? Is it a story evening, or dancing-school and games?"

"We had dancing-school last night," said the bear. "I have n't got over it yet. I backed into the fire twice in 'forward and back, and cross over.' Let us have a story to-night."

"Yes!" said the grandmother. "It is just the night for a story; and if you wish it, I will tell you one myself."

" Oh ! please, Madam ! " " Thank you, Madam ! " " Hurrah ! Granny ! " resounded on all sides, for the grandmother's stories were very popular; so, settling herself back in her chair, and beginning a new row in her knitting, the good woman said : —

" This story was told to me by my own grandmother. A story that has been told by two grandmothers in succession is supposed to be always true; you may therefore believe as much of this as you like."

And without further preface, she began as follows : —

CHAPTER II.

THE STORY OF CHOP-CHIN AND THE GOLDEN DRAGON.

ONCE upon a time, long ago and long ago, there lived in Pekin, which, as you all know, is the chief city of the Chinese Empire, a boy whose name was Chop-Chin. He was the son of Ly-Chee, a sweeper of the Imperial court-yard, whose duty it was to keep the pavement of the court-yard always absolutely clean, in case His Celestial Majesty, the Emperor, should feel inclined to put his celestial and majestic nose out-of-doors. Chop-Chin hoped to become a sweeper also, when he was a little older; but at the time when my story begins he was only twelve years old, and the law required that all sweepers should have passed their fourteenth year. So Chop-Chin helped his mother about the house, — for he was a good boy, — carried his father's dinner to him, and made himself generally useful.

One day Chop-Chin entered the court-yard at the usual time, carrying a jar of rice on his head, and a melon in one hand. These were for his father's dinner, and setting them down in a shaded corner, on the cool white marble pavement, he looked about for his father. But Ly-Chee was nowhere to be seen. A group of sweepers stood at the farther end of the court-yard, talking together in a state of wild excitement, with many gestures. One of them drew his hand across his throat rapidly, and they all shuddered. Some one was to be killed, then? Chop-Chin wondered what it all meant. Suddenly one of the group caught sight of him, and at once they fell silent. Two or three, who were friends of his father, began to wring their hands and tear their clothes, and the oldest sweeper of all advanced solemnly toward the boy, holding out both his hands, with the palms downward, in token of sympathy.

"My son," he said, "what is man's life but a string of beads, which at one time or another must be broken? Shall the wise man disquiet himself whether more or fewer beads have passed over the hand?"

"What words are these?" cried Chop-Chin, alarmed, though he knew not why. "Why do you look and speak so strangely, Yow-Lay; and where is my father?"

The old sweeper led the boy to a stone bench, and bade him sit down beside him. "Thou knowest," he said, "that the first duty of us sweepers is to keep the court-yard always as clean as the sky after rain, and as white as the breath of the frost."

"I know it well," replied the boy. "Does not my father wear out two pairs of scrubbing-shoes in a month —"

"Scrubbing-shoes, Granny?" said Toto, softly. "I didn't mean to interrupt, but what *are* scrubbing-shoes?"

"I remember asking the same question at your age, Toto," said the old lady, "and my grandmother told me that the sweepers always wore shoes with very thick soles, in which stiff bristles were fastened as in a scrubbing-brush. It was their custom to dash the water in bucketfuls over the pavement, and then dance violently about, scrubbing with their feet as hard as they could."

"Oh, what fun!" cried Toto. "May n't we try it some day, Granny? I'll fasten four brushes to your feet, Coon, and you can scrub the floor every day."

"Thank you, kindly!" said the raccoon. "If you can get the brushes on my feet, I will pledge myself to dance in them. That is certainly fair."

He winked slyly at Toto, while the grandmother continued : —

"Alas! my son," said the old man, "your father will wear out no more scrubbing-shoes. Listen! This morning, while we were all busily at work, it chanced through some evil fate that His Celestial Majesty felt a desire to taste the freshness of the morning air. Unannounced he came, with only the Princely Parasol-Holder, the Unique .Umbrella-Opener, and seven boys to hold up his celestial train. You know that your father is slightly deaf? Yes. Well, he stood — my good friend Ly-Chee — he stood with his back to the palace. He heard not the noise of the opening door, and at the very moment when His Celestial Majesty stepped out into the court-yard, Ly-Chee cast a great bucketful of ice-cold water backward, with fatal force and precision."

Chop-Chin shuddered, and hid his face in his hands.

"Picture to yourself the dreadful scene!" continued the ancient sweeper. "The Celestial Petticoat, of yellow satin damask, was drenched. The Celestial Shoes, of chicken-skin embroidered in gold, were reduced to a pulp. A shriek burst from every mouth! Your unhappy father turned, and seeing what he had done, fell on his face, as did all the rest of us. In silence we waited for the awful voice, which presently said : —

"'Princely Parasol-Holder, our feet are wet.'

"The Princely Parasol-Holder groaned, and

chattered his teeth together to express his anguish.

"'Unique Umbrella-Opener,' continued the Emperor, 'our petticoat is completely saturated.'

"The Unique Umbrella-Opener tore his clothes, and shook his hair wildly about his face, with moans of agony.

"'Let this man's head be removed at sunrise to-morrow!' concluded His Celestial Majesty.

"Then we all, lying on our faces, wept and cried aloud, and besought the celestial mercy for our comrade. We told the Emperor of Ly-Chee's long and faithful service; of his upright and devout life; of his wife and children, who looked to him for their daily bread. But all was of no avail. He repeated, in dreadful tones, his former words:—

"'Our feet are wet. Our petticoat is saturated. Let this man's head be removed at sunrise to-morrow.'

"Then the Unique Umbrella-Holder, who is a kindly man, made also intercession for

Ly-Chee. But now the Emperor waxed wroth, and he said : —

" ' Are our clothes to be changed, or do we stand here all day in wetness because of this dog ? We swear that unless the Golden Dragon himself come down from his altar and beg for this man's life, he shall die ! Enough ! ' And with these words he withdrew into the palace.

· " So thou seest, my son," said the old man, sadly, " that all is over with thy poor father. He is now in the prison of the condemned, and to-morrow at sunrise he must die. Go home, boy, and comfort thy poor mother, telling her this sad thing as gently as thou mayest."

Chop-Chin arose, kissed the old man's hand in token of gratitude for his kindness, and left the court-yard without a word. His head was in a whirl, and strange thoughts darted through it. He went home, but did not tell his mother of the fate which awaited her husband on the morrow. He could not feel that it was true. It *could not be* that the

next day, all in a moment, his father would
cease to live. There must be some way, —
some way to save him. And then he seemed
to hear the dreadful words, " Unless the Gold-
en Dragon himself come down from his altar
and beg for this man's life, he shall die." He
told his mother, in answer to her anxious
questions, that his father meant to pass the
night in the court-yard, as he would be
wanted very early in the morning; and as
it was a hot day, and promised a warm
night, the good woman felt no uneasiness,
but turned again to her pots and pans.

But Chop-Chin sat on the bench in front
of the house, with his head in his hands
thinking deeply.

That evening, at sunset, a boy was seen
walking slowly along the well-paved street
which led to the great temple of the Gold-
en Dragon. He was clad in a snow-white
tunic falling to his knees; his arms and
legs were bare; and his pig-tail, unbraided
and hanging in a crinkly mass below his

waist, showed that he was bent on some sacred mission. In his hands, raised high above his head, he carried a bronze bowl of curious workmanship. Many people turned to look at the boy, for his face and figure were of singular beauty.

"He carries the prayers of some great prince," they said, "to offer at the shrine of the Golden. Dragon."

And, indeed, it was at the great bronze gate of the Temple that the boy stopped. Poising the bronze bowl gracefully on his head with one hand, with the other he knocked three times on the gate. It opened, and revealed four guards clad in black armor, who stood with glittering pikes crossed, their points towards the boy.

"What seekest thou," asked the leader, "in the court of the Holy Dragon?"

Chop-Chin (for I need not tell you the boy was he) lowered the bowl from his head, and offered it to the soldier with a graceful reverence.

"Tong-Ki-Tcheng," he said, "sends you

greeting, and a draught of cool wine. He begs your prayers to the Holy Dragon that he may recover from his grievous sickness, and prays that I may pass onward to the shrine."

The guards bowed low at the name of Tong-Ki-Tcheng, a powerful Prince of the Empire, who lay sick of a fever in his palace, as all the city knew. Each one in turn took a draught from the deep bowl, and the leader said : —

"Our prayers shall go up without ceasing for Tong-Ki-Tcheng, the noble and great. Pass on, fair youth, and good success go with thee!"

They lowered their pikes, and Chop-Chin passed slowly through the court-yard paved with black marble, and came to the second gate, which was of shining steel. Here he knocked again, and the gate was opened by four guards clad in steel from top to toe, and glittering in the evening light.

"What seekest thou," they asked, "in the court of the Holy Dragon?"

Chop-Chin answered as before : —

"Tong-Ki-Tcheng sends you greeting, and a draught of cool wine. He begs your prayers to the Holy Dragon that he may recover from his grievous sickness, and prays that I may pass onward to the shrine."

The guards drank deeply from the bowl, and their leader replied : "Our prayers shall not cease to go up for Tong-Ki-Tcheng. Pass on, and good success go with thee!"

Onward the boy went, holding the bronze bowl high above his head. He crossed the white marble court-yard, and his heart beat when he came to the third gate, which was of whitest ivory, for he knew that beyond the third court-yard was the Temple itself,—the House of Gold, in which dwelt the mighty Dragon, the most sacred idol in all China. He paused a moment, and then with a steady hand knocked at the gate. It opened without a sound, and there stood four guards in white armor inlaid with gold. The same questions and answers were repeated. They drank from the bowl, promised their prayers for Tong-Ki-Tcheng, and then bade the boy pass onward to the golden gate, which gleamed at the farther end of the court-yard.

"But see that thou touch not the gate!" said the chief soldier. "It is the gate of the Temple itself, and no profane hand may rest upon it. Speak only, and the priests will hear and open to thee."

Softly Chop-Chin paced across the last court, which was paved with blocks of ivory and silver, laid in cunning patterns. Halting before the gate of gold, he raised the bowl in his hands, and said softly:—

"Ka Ho Yai! Yai Nong Ti!
Tong-Ki-Tcheng Lo Hum Ki Ni!"

The gates opened, and showed four priests in robes of cloth-of-gold, with golden censers in hand.

"Rash youth!" said the chief priest, "by what right or by whose order comest thou here, to the Sacred Shrine of the Holy Dragon?"

Chop-Chin knelt upon the threshold of the golden gate, and, with bowed head and downcast eyes, held out the bronze bowl.

"By the right of mortal sickness, most holy priest, come I hither!" he said, "and by order of the noble Tong-Ki-Tcheng. He prays thee and thy brethren to drink to his recovery from his grievous malady, and that your prayers may go up with mine at the Jewelled Shrine itself."

The priest drank solemnly from the bowl, and handed it to his assistants, the last of whom drained the last drop of wine.

"Our prayers shall truly go up for Tong-Ki-Tcheng," he said. "Give me thy hand, fair youth, and I will lead thee to the Jewelled Shrine. But first I will cover thine eyes, for none save ourselves, priests of the First Order of the Saki-Pan, may look upon the face of the Holy Dragon."

So saying, he bound a silk handkerchief firmly over the boy's eyes, and taking his hand, led him slowly forward.

Chop-Chin's heart was beating so violently

that he was half suffocated. He felt the
floor suddenly cold, cold, beneath his feet,
and knew that he was walking on the golden
floor of the Temple. A few steps farther, the
hand of the priest drew him downward, and
together with the four priests he lay prostrate on his face before the shrine of the
Golden Dragon.

A great silence followed. The warm, incense-laden air was stirred by no sound save
the breathing of the five suppliants. No
breeze rustled the heavy satin curtains which
shrouded the windows; no hum of insect or
song of bird came from the outer world,
which was fast settling down into night.

Silence!

The boy Chop-Chin lay as still as if he
were carved in marble. He held his breath
from time to time, and his whole being
seemed strained to one effort, — that of listening. Did he hear anything? Was the
breathing of the four priests changing a
little, — growing deeper, growing louder?
There! and there again! was that a whisper

of prayer, or was it — could it be — the faintest suspicion of a snore? He lay still; waited and listened, listened and waited. After a little while there could be no doubt about it, — the four men were breathing heavily, slowly, regularly; and one of them rolled out a sonorous, a majestic snore, which resounded through the heavy perfumed air of the Temple, yet caused no movement among the other three. There could be no doubt about it, — the priests were asleep!

Slowly, softly, the boy lifted his head; then he rose to his knees, and looked fearfully at the sleepers. There they lay, flat on their faces, their hands clasped over their heads. He touched one of them, — there was no answering movement. He shook another by the shoulders; he shook them all. They snored in concert, but gave no other sign of life. The drugged wine had done its work.

Then, and not till then, did Chop-Chin venture to lift his eyes and look upon the awful mystery which was hidden by these golden walls. He trembled, he turned white as the tunic which covered his dusky limbs; but standing erect, he gazed firmly at the Golden Dragon. From the floor rose a splendid altar of gold, studded thick with precious gems. Rubies, sapphires, and emeralds, set in mystic lines and figures, formed the characters which told the thirty-two names of the world-renowned dragon; and on the top of this glittering pedestal, fifteen feet in the air, stood the idol itself.

It was, indeed, a marvellous thing to look upon. Ten feet long, composed entirely of thin scales of the purest gold, laid over and over each other, and each scale tipped with a diamond. Two magnificent rubies glowed in the eye-sockets, and the head was surmounted by a crown of emeralds worth any ordinary kingdom. But the tail! the tail was the wonder of wonders. Millions of delicate gold wires as fine as silk waved gracefully from the scaly tip a length of three feet, and each one was tipped with a diamond, a ruby, or an emerald of surpassing beauty and lustre. So wonderful was the shimmering light of the stones that the whole tail seemed to sway and curl to and fro, as if some living creature were moving it, and rays of rainbow-colored light darted from it on every side, dazzling the eyes of the beholder.

Chop-Chin gazed and gazed, and hid his eyes and trembled, and gazed again. At last he shook himself together, and whispered, " My father! my father!" Then softly, surely, he began to climb up the golden altar. Stepping carefully from glittering point to point, holding on here by a projecting ornament of carven amethyst, there by a block of jasper or onyx, he reached the top; then steadying himself, he leaned forward and lifted the Holy Dragon from its stand. To his amazement, instead of being barely able to move it, he found he could easily carry it, for the golden plates which formed it were so delicate that the weight of the whole great creature was incredibly small. Lightly the boy lifted it in his arms, and slowly, surely, noiselessly bore it to the ground. Here he paused, and looked keenly at the sleeping priests. Did that one's eyelids quiver; did his mouth twitch, as if he were waking from his sleep? Was that a movement of yon other man's arm, as if he were stealthily preparing to rise, to spring upon the sacrilegious robber? No! it was but the play of the colored light on the faces and raiment of the sleepers. The voice of their snoring still went up, calmly, evenly, regularly. The wine had done its work well.

Then Chop-Chin took off the sash which bound his tunic at the waist, and shook out its folds. It was a web of crimson silk, so fine and soft that it could be drawn through a finger-ring, and yet, when spread out, so ample that the boy found no difficulty in completely covering with it his formidable prize. Thus enwrapped, he bore the Golden Dragon swiftly from the Temple, closing the doors of gold softly behind him. He crossed the ivory and silver pavement of the inner court, and came to the ivory gate. It was closed, and beside it lay the four white-clad warriors, sunk in profound slumber. Stepping lightly over their prostrate forms, Chop-Chin opened the gate softly, and found himself in the second court. This, also, he traversed safely, finding the armed guardians of the steel gate also sleeping soundly, with their mouths wide open, and their shining spears pointing valiantly at nothing. A touch upon the glittering gate, — it opened, and Chop-Chin began to breathe more freely when he saw the bronze gates of the outer court-yard, and knew that in another minute, if all went well, he would be in the open street. But, alas! the four guards clad in black armor, who kept watch by the outer gate, had been the first to drink the drugged wine, and already the effect of the powerful narcotic which it contained had begun to wear off. As Chop-Chin, bearing in his arms the shrouded figure of the mighty idol, approached the gate, one of the four sleepers stirred, yawned, rubbed his eyes, and looked about him. It was quite dark, but his eye caught the faint glimmer of the boy's white robe, and seizing his pike, he exclaimed, —

"Who goes there?"

Chop-Chin instantly stepped to his side, and said in a low whisper, —

"It is I, Nai-Ping, second priest of the Saki-Pan, bound on business of the Temple. Let me pass, and quickly, for the chief priest waits my return."

The sentinel bowed low, and undid the fastenings of the huge bronze gates. They swung open silently, and the boy passed through with his awful burden.

"Strange!" soliloquized the guard, as he drew the massive bolts again. "I never knew one of the priests to go out at this time of night. But I dared not say anything, lest he should find out that I was asleep at my post. And now that he is gone," he added, "I may as well just take forty winks, as he may be away some time."

So saying, he curled himself up on the marble pavement, and fell this time into a natural slumber.

Ten o'clock of a dark night. The outer gates of the royal palace were closed, though lights still shone in many of the windows. Outside the gate a sentinel was pacing up and down, armed with pike and broadsword. Every time he turned on his beat, he looked up and down the narrow street to see if anything or anybody were approaching. Suddenly, as he wheeled about, he saw before him a figure which seemed to have sprung all in a moment out of the blackness of the night. It was the figure of a boy, carrying a burden considerably larger than himself, — a dark and shapeless mass, which yet seemed not to be heavy in proportion to its size.

"What is this?" cried the astonished sentinel. "Who art thou, and what monstrous burden is this thou carriest so lightly?"

"Hist!" said the boy, speaking in an awe-struck whisper, "speak not so loud, friend! This is the Celestial Footstool!"

The sentinel recoiled, and stared in dismay at the dark bundle.

"May the Holy Dragon preserve me!" he said. "What has happened?"

"His Celestial Majesty," replied Chop-Chin, "threw it in anger at his Putter-on-of-Slippers yesterday, and broke one of its legs. All day my master, the Chief Cabinet-maker, has been at work on it, and now he has sent me with it by nightfall, that no profane eye may see clearly even the outer covering of the sacred object."

"Pass in," said the sentinel, opening the gate. "But tell me, knowest thou how it will fare with the Putter-on-of-Slippers? He is cousin to my stepfather's aunt by marriage, and I would not that aught of ill should befall so near a relative.

"Alas! I know not," said the boy, hastening forward. "I fear it may go hard with him."

The sentinel shook his head sadly, and resumed his walk; while Chop-Chin crept softly through the court-yard, keeping close to the wall, and feeling as he went along for a certain little door he knew of, which led by a staircase cut in the thickness of the wall to a certain unused closet, near the Celestial Bed-chamber. -

While all this was going on, the Emperor of China, the great and mighty Wah-Song, was going to bed. He had sipped his night-draught of hot wine mingled with honey and spices, sitting on the edge of the Celestial Bed, with the Celestial Nightcap of cloth-of-silver tied comfortably under his chin, and the Celestial Dressing-gown wrapped around him. He had scolded the Chief Pillow-thumper because the pillows were not ·fat enough, and because there were only ten of them instead of twelve. He had boxed the ears of the Tyer-of-the-Strings-of-the-Nightcap, and had thrown his golden goblet at the Principal Pourer, who brought him the wine. And when all these things were done, his Celestial Majesty Wah-Song got into bed, and was tucked in by the Finishing Toucher, who got his nose well tweaked by way of thanks. Then the taper of perfumed wax was lighted, and the shade of alabaster put over it, and then the other lights were extinguished; and then the attendants all crawled out backwards on their hands and knees, and shut the door after them; and then His Celestial Majesty went to sleep.

Peacefully the Emperor slept, — one hour, two hours, three hours, — discoursing eloquently the while in the common language of mankind, — the language of the nose. At last he began to dream, — a dreadful dream. He was in the Golden Temple, praying before the Jewelled Shrine. He heard an awful voice, — the voice of the Golden Dragon. It called his name; it glared upon him with its ruby eyes; it lifted its crowned head, and stretched its long talons toward him. Ah! ah! The Emperor tried to scream, but he could make no sound. Once more the dreadful voice was heard: —

"Wah-Song! Wah-Song! Awake!"

The Emperor sprang up in bed, and looked about him with eyes wild with terror. Ah! what was that? — that glittering form standing at the foot of his bed; that crowned head raised high as if in anger; those

At last the Emperor began to dream. He heard an awful voice, the voice
of the Golden Dragon. "Wah-song! Wah-song! Awake!" — PAGE 44.

glaring red eyes fixed menacingly upon him!

"Ah, horror! ah, destruction! the Golden Dragon is here!"

With one long howl of terror and anguish, His Celestial Majesty Wah-Song rolled off the bed and under it, in one single motion, and lay there flat on his face, with his hands clasped over his head. Quaking in every limb, his teeth chattering, and a cold sweat pouring from him, he listened as the awful voice spoke again.

"Wah-Song!" said the Golden Dragon, "thou hast summoned me, and I am here!"

The wretched Emperor moaned.

"I — I — I sum-summon thee, most Golden and Holy Dragon?" he stammered faintly. "May I be b-b-bastinadoed if I did!"

"Listen!" said the Dragon, sternly, "and venture not to speak save when I ask thee a question. Yesterday morning, in consequence of thine own caprice in going out unannounced, thy silly shoes and thy pusillanimous petticoat became wet. For this nothing, thou has condemned to death my faithful servant Ly-Chee, who has brought me fresh melons every Tuesday afternoon for thirty years. When others, less inhuman than thou, interceded for his life, thou madest reply, 'We swear, that unless the Golden Dragon himself come down from his altar and beg for this man's life, he shall die!'"

The Emperor groaned, and clawed the carpet in his anguish.

"Therefore, Wah-Song," continued the Dragon, "I AM HERE! I come not to beg, but to command. Dost thou hear me?"

"Ye-ye-yes!" murmured the wretched monarch. "I hear thee, Most Mighty. I — I — did n't know he brought thee melons. I brought thee two dozen pineapples myself, the other day," he added piteously.

"Thou didst!" exclaimed the Golden Dragon, fiercely. "Thou didst, *slave!* and they were half-rotten. HA!" and he gave a little jump on the floor, making his glittering tail wave, and his flaming eyes glared yet more fiercely at the unfortunate Wah-

Song, who clung yet more closely to the carpet, and drummed on it with his heels in an extremity of fear.

"Listen, now," said the Fiery Idol, "to my commañds. Before day-break thou wilt send a free pardon to Ly-Chee, who now lies in the prison of the condemned, expecting to die at sunrise."

"I will! I will!" cried the Emperor.

"Moreover," continued the Dragon, "thou wilt send him, by a trusty messenger, twenty bags of goodly ducats, one for every hour that he has spent in prison."

The Emperor moaned feebly, for he loved his goodly ducats.

"Furthermore, thou wilt make Ly-Chee thy Chief Sweeper for life, with six brooms of gilded straw, with ivory handles, as his yearly perquisite, besides three dozen pairs of scrubbing-shoes; and his son, Chop-Chin, shalt thou appoint as Second Sweeper, to help his father."

The Emperor moaned again, but very faintly, for he dared not make any objection.

"These are my orders!" continued the Dragon. "Obey them strictly and speedily, and thine offence may be pardoned. Neglect them, even in the smallest particular, and — Ha! Hum! Wurra-*wurra*-G-R-R-R-R-R-R!" and here the Dragon opened his great red mouth, and uttered so fearful a growl that the miserable Emperor lost hold of such little wits as had remained to him, and fainted dead away.

Ten minutes later, the sentinel at the gate was amazed at the sight of the Chief Cabinet-maker's apprentice, reappearing suddenly before him, with his monstrous burden still in his arms. The boy's hair was dishevelled, and his face was very pale. In truth, it had been very hard work to get in and out of the hollow golden monster, and Chop-Chin was well-nigh exhausted by his efforts, and the great excitement which had nerved him to carry out his bold venture.

"How now!" cried the sentinel. "What means this, boy?"

"Alas!" said Chop-Chin, "alas! unhappy that I am! Was it my fault that the mended leg was a hair-breadth shorter than the others? Good soldier, I have been most grievously belabored, even with the Sacred Footstool itself, which, although it be a great honor, is nevertheless a painful one. And now must I take it back to my master, for it broke again the last time His Celestial Majesty brought it down on my head. Wherefore let me pass, good, sentinel, for I can hardly stand for weariness."

"Pass on, poor lad!" said the good-natured soldier. "And yet — stay a moment! thinkest thou that aught would be amiss if I were to take just one peep at the Celestial Footstool? Often have I heard of its marvellous workmanship, and its tracery of pearl and ebony. Do but lift one corner of the mantle, good youth, and let me see at least a leg of the wonder."

"At thy peril, touch it not!" cried the boy, in great alarm. "Knowest thou not that the penalty is four hundred lashes?

Not a single glance have I ventured to cast at it, for they say its color changes if any profane eye rest upon its polished surface."

"Pass on, then, in the name of the Dragon!" said the sentinel, opening the gate; and bidding him a hasty good-night, Chop-Chin hurried away into the darkness.

Now, while all this was going on, it chanced that the four priests of the First Order of the Saki-Pan awoke from their slumber. What their feelings were when they lifted their eyes and saw that the Golden Dragon was gone, is beyond my power to tell. Their terror was so extreme that they did not dare to move, but after the first horrified glance at the bare altar flung themselves flat on their faces again, and howled and moaned in their anguish.

"We slept!" they cried, in a doleful chant of misery. "Yea, verily slept we.

"Ai! ai! we know not why;
Wow! wow! we know not how.

"Thou removedst thyself. Thou raisedst the paw of strength and the hind-feet of swiftness. Because we slept, thou hast gone away, and we are desolate, awaiting the speedily-advancing death.

"Hong! Kong! Punka-wunka-woggle!
Hong! Kong! Punka-wunka-wogg!"

While thus the wretched priests lay on the golden floor, bewailing their sin and its dreadful consequences, there fell suddenly on their ears a loud and heavy sound. It was at some distance, — a heavy clang, as of some one striking on metal. "Pong! pong!" what could it be? And now came other sounds, — the opening and shutting of gates, the tread of hasty feet, the sound of hurried voices, and finally a loud knocking at the door of the Temple itself.

"Open, most holy Priests of the Saki-Pan!" cried a voice. "We have strange and fearful news! Open without delay!"

The unhappy priests hurried to the door, and flung it open with trembling hands. Without stood all the guards of all the gates,

the white and the steel-clad soldiers cluster-
ing about the four black-clad guardians of
the outer gate.

"Speak!" said the chief priest in great
agitation, "what is your errand?"

"O Priest!" said the black guards, trembling with excitement, "we heard a great
knocking at the gate."

"Yes, yes!" cried the priest, "I know
it. What more?"

"O Priest!" said the guards, "we were
affrighted, so great was the noise; so we
opened the gate but a little way, and peeped
through; and we saw — we saw —" They
paused, and gasped for breath.

"Speak, sons of pigs!" shrieked the priest,
"*what* did you see?"

"We saw the Golden Dragon!" said the
soldiers, in a fearful whisper. "He is sitting
up — on his hind-legs — with his mouth open!
and he knocked — he knocked —"

But the priests of the Saki-Pan waited to
hear no more. Rushing through the court-
yards, they flung wide open the great bronze

gates. They caught up the Golden Dragon, they raised it high on their shoulders, and with shouts of rejoicing they bore it back to the Temple, while the guards prostrated themselves before it.

"He went out!" sang the priests. "He walked abroad, for the glory and welfare of his subjects. He cast upon the city the eye of beneficence; he waved over it the pleni-potentiary tail!

> "Ai! ai! we know not why!
> Wow! wow! we know not how!

Glory to the Holy Dragon, and happiness and peace to the city and the people!"

But in the house of Ly-Chee all was sun-shine and rejoicing, At daybreak a pro-cession had come down the little street, — a troop of soldiers in the imperial uniform, with music sounding before them, and gay banners flaunting in the morning air. In the midst of the troop rode Ly-Chee, on a splendid black horse. He was dressed in a robe of crimson satin embroidered with gold, and round his neck hung strings of jewels most glorious to see. Behind him walked twenty slaves, each carrying a fat bag of golden ducats; and after the troop came more slaves, bearing gilded brooms with ivory handles and scrubbing-shoes of the finest quality. And all the soldiers and all the slaves cried aloud, continually: —

"Honor to Ly-Chee, the Chief-Sweeper of the court-yard! Honor and peace to him and all his house!"

The procession stopped before the little house, and the good sweeper, stupefied still with astonishment at his wonderful good fortune, dismounted and clasped his wife and children in his arms. And they wept together for joy, and the soldiers and the slaves and all the people wept with them.

But the Celestial Emperor, Wah-Song, lay in bed for two weeks, speaking to no man, and eating nothing but water-gruel. And when he arose, at the end of that time, behold! he was as meek as a six-years old child.

CHAPTER III.

THE grandmother's story was received with great approbation, and the different members of the family commented on it, each after his fashion.

"I should like to have been Chop-Chin!" exclaimed Toto. "How exciting it must have been! Only think, Coon, of talking to the Emperor in that way, and scolding him as if he were a little boy."

"Well, I never saw an Emperor," said the raccoon; "but I certainly should not wish to talk to one, if they are all such wretched creatures as Wah-Song. *I* should like to have been the Finishing-Toucher; then if he had pulled *my* nose — hum! ha! we should see!"

"Dear Madam," said the bear, who had been staring meditatively into the fire, "there is one thing in the story that I do not understand; that is — well — you spoke of the boy's having a pig-tail."

"Yes, Bruin!" said the grandmother. "A Chinese pig-tail, you know."

"Yes, certainly," said Bruin. "A Chinese pig's tail it would naturally be. Now, I confess I do not see *how* a pig's tail could be worn on the head, or how it could be unbraided; that is, if the Chinese pigs have tails like that of our friend in the sty yonder."

Toto laughed aloud at this, and even the grandmother could not help smiling a very little; but she gently told Bruin what a Chinaman's pig-tail was, and how he wore it. Meantime, Miss Mary, the parrot, looked on with an air of dignified amusement.

"My respected father," she said presently, "spent some years in China. It is a fine country, though too far from Africa for my taste."

"Tell us about your father, Miss Mary!" exclaimed the squirrel. "Fine old bird he must have been, eh?"

"He was, indeed!" replied the parrot, with some emotion. "He was a noble bird. His beak, which I am said to have inherited, was the envy of every parrot in Central Africa. He could whistle in nine languages, and his tail — but as the famous poet Gabblio has sweetly sung, —

> "'All languages and tongues must fail,
> In speaking of Polacko's tail.'

"Polacko was my father's name," she explained. "He was universally respected. Ah, me!"

"But how came he to go to China?" asked Toto.

"He was captured, my dear, and taken there when very young. He lived there for twenty years, with one of the chief mandarins of the empire. He led a happy life, with a perch and ring of ebony and silver, the freedom of the house, and chow-chow four times a day. At last, however, the young grandson of the mandarin insisted upon my father's learning to eat with chopsticks. The lofty spirit of Polacko could not brook this outrage, and the door being left open one day he flew away and made his way to Africa, the home of his infancy, where he passed the rest of his life. I drop a tear," added Miss Mary, raising her claw gracefully to her eyes, " to his respected memory."

Nobody saw the tear, but all looked grave and sympathetic, and the good-natured bear said, " Quite right, I'm sure. Very proper, certainly ! "

But now the grandmother rose and folded up her knitting.

"Dear friends, and Toto, boy," she said, " it is bed-time, now, for the clock has struck nine. Good-night, and pleasant dreams to you all. My good Bruin, you will cover the fire, and lock up the house ? "

" Trust me for that, dear Madam ! " said the bear, heartily.

" Come, then, Cracker," said the old lady. " Your basket is all ready for you, and it is high time you were in it." And with the squirrel perched on her shoulder she went into her own little room, closing the door behind her.

After exchanging mutual "good-nights," the other members of the family sought their respective sleeping-places. The birds flew to their perches, and each, tucking her head and one leg away in some mysterious manner, became suddenly a very queer-looking creature indeed.

"Coon," said Toto, "come and sleep on my bed, won't you? My feet were cold, last night, and you do make such a delightful foot-warmer."

"Humph!" said the raccoon, doubtfully. "I don't know, Toto. It won't be as warm for *me* as my basket, though no doubt it would be nice for you."

"I'll put the big blue dressing-gown over you," said Toto. "You know you like that, because you can put your nose in the pocket, and keep it warm."

"All right," cried the raccoon. "Come along, then!" and off they went.

Bruin now proceeded to rake the ashes over the fire, covering it neatly and carefully. He filled the kettle; he drew the bolts of door and windows; and finally, when all was snug and safe, the good bear laid himself down on the hearth-rug, and soon was fast asleep.

Now all was quiet in the little cottage. Outside, the snow still fell, softly, steadily, silently. In the shed, Bridget, the cow, was sleeping soundly, with a cock and three hens roosting on her back, according to their invariable custom. In the warm, covered sty the pig also slept. He had no name, the pig; he would have scorned one.

"I am a pig," he was wont to say, "and as such every one knows me. There is no danger of my being mistaken for anything else." Which was very true.

But though slumber held fast, apparently, all the dwellers in cottage, shed, and sty, there were in reality two pairs of eyes which were particularly wide-awake at this moment. They were very black eyes, very bright eyes, and they were, if you wish to know, peeping into the kitchen through the crack under the cellar-door, to see what they could see.

"Nobody there!" said little brown Squeak.

"No, nobody there!" said little brown Scrabble.

"Hark! what was that noise?" cried Squeak.

"Only the wind!" said Scrabble.

"Do you think we can get through the crack?" said Squeak.

"Nothing like trying!" said Scrabble.

"Scrabble!" went little brown Squeak.

"Squeak!" went little brown Scrabble.

And the next moment they were in the kitchen.

It was nearly dark, but not quite, for the covered embers still sent out a dusky glow. It was warm; the floor was smooth and flat; there was a smell as if there might be something to eat, somewhere. Altogether, it was a very pleasant place for two little mice to play in; and as they had it all to themselves, why should they not play? Play they did, therefore, with right good-will; scampering hither and thither, rolling over and over each other, poking their little sharp noses into every crack and cranny they could find. Oh, what fun it was! How smooth the floor! how pleasant the dry, warm air, after their damp cellar-home!

But about that smell, now! where did it come from? Playing and romping is hungry work, and the two little brown mouse-stomachs are empty. It seems to come from under that cupboard door. The crack is wide enough to let out the smell, but not quite wide enough to let in Messrs. Scrabble and Squeak. If they could enlarge it a bit, now, with the sharp little tools which they always carry in their mouths! So said, so done! - "Nibble! nibble! nibble! Gnaw! gnaw! gnaw!" It is very fatiguing work; but, see! the crack widens. If one made oneself *very* small, now? It is done, and the two mice find themselves in the immediate neighborhood of a large piece of squash pie. Oh, joy! oh, delight! too great for speech or squeak,

but just right for attack. " Nibble ! nibble !
Gobble ! gobble ! " and soon the plate shines
white and empty, with only the smell of the
roses — I mean the pie — clinging round it
still. There is nothing else to eat in the
cupboard, is there ? Yes ! what is this paper
package which smells so divinely, sending
a warm, spicy, pungent fragrance through
the air ? Ah ! pie was good, but this will be
better ! Nibble through the paper quickly,
and then — Alas ! alas ! the spicy fragrance
means *ginger*, and it is not only warm, but
hot. Oh, it burns ! oh, it scorches ! fire is in
our mouths, in our noses, our throats, our little brown stomachs, now only too well filled.
Water ! water ! or we die, and never see our
cool, beloved cellar again. Hurry down from
the shelf, creep through the crack, rush frantically round the kitchen. Surely there is a
smell of water ? Yes, yes ! there it is, in
that tin basin, yonder. Into it we go, splash-
ing, dashing, drinking in the silver coolness,
washing this fiery torment from our mouths
and throats.

Thoroughly sobered by this adventure, the two little mice sat on the floor beside the basin, dripping and shivering, the water trickling from their long tails, their short ears, their sharp-pointed noses. They blinked sadly at each other with their bright black eyes.

"Shall we go home now, Scrabble?" said Squeak. "It is late, and Mother Mouse will be looking for us."

"I'm so c-c-c-cold!" shivered Scrabble, who a moment before had been devoured by burning heat. "Don't you think we might dry ourselves before that fire before we go down?"

"Yes!" replied Squeak, "we will. But — what is that great black thing in front of the fire?"

"A hill, of course!" said the other. "A black hill, I should say. Shall we climb over it, or go round it?"

"Oh, let us climb over it!" said Squeak. "The exercise will help to warm us; and it is such a queer-looking hill, I want to explore it."

So they began to climb up the vast black mass, which occupied the whole space in front of the fireplace.

"How soft the ground is! and it is warm, too!"

"Because it is near the fire, stupid!"

"And what is this tall black stuff that grows so thick all over it? It isn't a bit like grass, or trees either."

"It *is* grass, of course, stupid! what else could it be? Come on! come on! we are nearly at the top, now."

"Scrabble," said little brown Squeak, stopping short, "you may call me stupid as much as you please, but *I* don't like this place. I— I— I think it is moving."

"*Moving?*" said little brown Scrabble, in a tone of horror.

And then the two little mice clutched each other with their little paws, and wound their little tails round each other, and held on tight, tight, for the black mass *was* moving! There was a long, stretching, undulating movement, slow but strong; and then came a quick, violent, awful shake, which sent the two brothers slipping, sliding, tumbling headlong to the floor. Picking themselves up as well as they could, and casting one glance back at the black hill, they rushed shrieking and squeaking to the cellar-door, and literally flung themselves through the crack. For in that glance they had seen a vast red cavern, a yawning gulf of fire, open suddenly in the black mass, which was now heaving and shuddering all over. And from this fiery cavern came smoke and flame (at least so the mice said when they got home to the maternal hole), and an awful roaring sound, which shook the whole house and made the windows rattle.

"Home to our Mother Mouse! Home to our Mother Mouse! and never, never, will we leave our cellar again!"

But Bruin sat up on his haunches, and scratched himself and stretched himself, and gave another mighty yawn.

"Haw-wa-wow-you-*wonk!*" said the good bear. "Those must have been very lively fleas, to wake me out of a sound sleep. I wonder where they have crept to! I don't seem to feel them now. Ha! humph! Ya-ow! very sleepy! Not morning yet; take another nap."

And stretching his huge length once more along the floor, Bruin slept again.

CHAPTER IV.

AT dinner the next day, it was noticed that Coon was very melancholy. He shook his head frequently, and sighed so deeply and sorrowfully that the kind heart of the wood-pigeon was moved to pity.

"Are you not well, my dear Coon?" she asked. "Something has gone amiss with you, evidently. Tell us what it is."

The raccoon shook his head again, and looked unutterably doleful.

"I knew how it would be, Coon," said the bear. "You should n't have eaten that third pie for supper. Two pies are enough for anybody, after such a quantity of bread and honey and milk as you had."

Coon sighed again, more deeply than before.

"I *did n't* eat it all," he said; "I only wish I had!"

"Why, Coon," queried Toto, "what's the trouble?"

"Well," said Coon, "there was a piece left. I could n't eat any more, so I put it away in the cupboard, thinking I would have it for lunch to-day. It was a lovely piece. I never saw such a squash pie as that was, anyhow, and that piece —"

He paused, and seemed lost in the thought of the pie.

"*Well!*" exclaimed Toto. "So you *did* eat it for your lunch, and now you are unhappy because you did n't keep it for dinner. Is that it?"

"Not at all!" replied the other, "not at all! I trust I am not *greedy*, Toto, *whatever* my faults may be. I went to get it for my luncheon, for I had been working all the morning like a —"

"Dormouse!"

"Tree-toad!"

"Grasshopper!" murmured the squirrel, the bear, and Toto, simultaneously.

"Like a RACCOON!" he continued severely.

"I can say no more than that; and I was desperately hungry. I went to the cupboard to get my piece of pie, and it was — gone!"

"Gone!" exclaimed the grandmother; "why, who can have taken it?"

"That is the point, Madam!" said Coon. "It was some small creature, for it got in through the crack under the cupboard door, gnawing away the wood. I have examined the marks," he added, "and they are the marks of small, very sharp teeth." And he looked significantly at the squirrel.

"What do you mean by looking at me in that way?" demanded little Cracker, whisking his tail fiercely, and bristling all over. "I've a good mind to bite your ears with my sharp teeth. I never touched your old pie. If you say I did, I'll throw this cheese —"

"Cracker! Cracker!" said the grandmother, gently, "you forget yourself! Good manners at table, you know. I am sure," she added, as Cracker hung his head and looked much ashamed, "that none of us think seriously for a moment that you took the pie. Coon loves his joke; but he has a good heart, and he would not really give you pain, I know. Of course he did not mean anything. Am I not right, Coon?"

It is only justice to the raccoon to say that he was rather abashed at this. He rubbed his nose, and gave a deprecatory wink at Bruin, who was looking very serious; then, recovering himself, he beamed expansively on the squirrel, who still looked fierce, though respect for "Madam" kept him silent.

"Mean anything?" he cried. "Dear Madam, do I *ever* mean anything, — anything unkind, at least?" he added hastily, as Toto looked up with a suppressed chuckle. "I beg your pardon, Cracker, my boy, and I hope you won't bear malice. As for those marks — "

"Those marks," interrupted the bear, who had risen from his seat and was examining the cupboard door, "were made by mice. I am quite sure of it."

"So am I," said Miss Mary, quietly. "I saw them do it."

"What!"

"You!"

"When?"

"How?"

"Tell us!" exclaimed every one, in a breath.

"Two brown mice," said Miss Mary, "came out from under the cellar-door about midnight. They gnawed at the cupboard till they had made the crack wide enough to pass through. Then I heard them say, 'Squash pie!' and heard them nibbling, or rather gobbling. After a while they came rushing out as if the cat were after them, and jumped into the water-basin. Then they tried to climb up Bruin's back, but he yawned like an alligator, and shook them off, and they ran hurry-scurry under the cellar-door again."

A great laugh broke out at this recital of Messrs. Squeak and Scrabble's nocturnal adventure, and under cover of the laughter the raccoon approached the parrot.

"Why didn't you give the alarm," he

asked, " or drive off the mice yourself? You knew it was my pie, for you saw me put it there."

Miss Mary cocked her bright yellow eye at him expressively.

"I lost two feathers from my tail, yesterday," she said. "Somebody bit them off while I was asleep. They were fine feathers, and I cannot replace them."

The two exchanged a long, deep look. At length —

"Miss Mary," said the raccoon aloud, "what was the color of your lamented husband? You told us once, but I am ashamed to say I'm not positive that I remember."

" Green ! " replied Miss Mary, in some surprise, — " a remarkably fine emerald green. But why do you ask ? "

" Ah, I thought so ! " said the raccoon, ingenuously. " That explains his choice of a wife. — Walk, Toto, did you say ? I am with you, my boy ! " and in three bounds he was out of the door, and leaping and frolicking about in the new-fallen snow.

Toto caught up his cap and followed him, and the two together made their way out of the yard, and walked, ran, leaped, jumped, tumbled, scrambled, toward the forest. The sky had cleared, and the sun shone brilliantly on the fresh white world. On every hand lay the snow, — here heaped and piled in fantastic drifts and strange half-human shapes; there spread smooth, like a vast counterpane. The tall trees of the forest bent under white feathery masses, which came tumbling down on Toto and his companion, as they lightly pushed the branches aside and entered the woods.

A winter walk in the woods! It is always a good thing for any one who has eyes in his head, but it is especially good when you see all that Coon and Toto saw; when you know, from every tiny track or footmark, what little creatures have been running or hopping about; when many of these little creatures are your friends, and all of them at least acquaintances. How fresh and crisp the air was! how soft and powdery and generally delightful the snow! What a pleasant world it was, on the whole!

"Let me see!" said the raccoon, stopping and looking about him. "It is just about here that Chucky's aunt lives. Yes, I remember, now. You see that oak-stump yonder, with the moss on it? Well, her burrow is just under that. Suppose we give her a call, and tell her how her hopeful nephew is."

"Nonsense!" said Toto, "she is as fast asleep as he is, of course. We could n't wake her if we tried, and why should we try?"

"Might have a game of ball with her," suggested the raccoon. "But I don't know that it 's worth while, after all."

"Who lives in that hollow tree, now?" asked Toto. "The wild-cat used to live there, you know. It is a very comfortable tree, if I remember right."

"You found it so once, did n't you, Toto?" said Coon. "Do you remember that day, when a thunder-shower came up, and you crept into that hollow tree for shelter?

Ha! ha! ha! *do* you remember that day, my boy?"

"I should think I did remember it!" cried Toto. "I am not likely to forget it. It was raining guns and pitchforks, and the lightning was cracking and zigzagging all through the forest, it seemed, and the thunder crashing and bellowing and roaring —"

"Like Bruin, when the bumble-bee stung his nose!" put in the raccoon.

"Exactly!" said Toto. "There I was, curled up well in the hollow, thinking how lucky I was, when suddenly came two green eyes glowering at me, and a great spitting and spluttering and meowling.

"'Get out of my house!' said the creature. 'F-s-s-s-s-yeh-yow-s-s-s-s-s-s! get out of my house, I say!'

"'My dear Madam,' I said, 'it is really more than you can expect. You are already thoroughly wet, and if you come here you will only drip all over the nice dry hole and spoil it. Now, *I* am quite dry; and to tell you the truth, I mean to remain so.'

" Oh, how angry that cat was!

" ' My name is Klawtobitz!' she cried. 'I have lived in this tree for seven years, and I am not going to be turned out of it by a thing with two legs and no tail. Who are you, I say?'

" ' I am a boy!' cried I, getting angry in my turn. 'I would n't have a tail if I was paid for it; and I will *not* leave this hole!'

" And then the old cat humped her back, and grinned till I saw every tooth in her head, and came flying at me, — claws spread, and tail as big round as my arm. There we fought, tooth and nail, fist and claw, till we were both out of breath. Finally I got her by the throat, and she made her teeth meet in my arm, and there we both were. I had heard no noise save the cat's screeching in my ear; but now, suddenly, a great growly voice, close beside us, cried, —

" ' Fair play! fair play! no choking!'

" We both dropped our hold, and looking up, saw — "

" Bruin and me! " interrupted the raccoon,

joyously. "We were taking a quiet prowl in the rain, and hearing the scuffle, stopped to see what was going on. Such a pretty fight I had not seen in a long time, and it was really too bad of Bruin to stop it. How old Ma'am Wildcat's tail went down, though, when she saw him!"

"I am very glad he did stop it," said Toto. "I was quite a little chap then, you see, — only seven years old, — and it was going hard with me. I was frightened enough, though, I can tell you, when I saw Bruin standing there. He looked as big as an elephant, and I fully expected to be eaten up the next minute. But he said, in his great hearty voice, —

"'Give us your paw, my little fighting-cock! And you, Mrs. Wildcat, be off! I gave you warning a week ago, when you killed the wood-pigeon's nestlings. Off with you, now, quick, or — '"

"And she went!" cried Coon. "Oh, yes, my dear, she went! And I went after her! I chased that cat for ten miles, to the very farthest end of the forest. She had the start of me, and kept it pretty well, but I was just overhauling her when we came to the open; she gave a flying leap from the last tree, and went crash through the window of a farm-house which stood close at hand! I thought she would probably be attended to there; so I went back, and found Bruin and you as sociable and friendly as if you had been brought up in the same den, — you sitting in the hole, with your funny red legs hanging out (you were the queerest-looking animal I had ever seen, Toto!), and he sitting up on his haunches, talking to you."

"And he invited us both to supper!" cried Toto. "Don't you remember, Coon? That was the first time I had ever seen any of you people, and I was dreadfully afraid that I should be the supper myself. But we went to his den, and had a jolly supper. Bruin ate three large watermelons, I remember. He *said* a man gave them to him."

"I think it very likely that he did," said Coon, "if Bruin asked him."

"And I showed you how to play leap-frog," continued Toto; "and we played it over Bruin's back till it was time for me to go home. And then you both walked with me to the edge of the forest, and there we swore eternal friendship."

"Ah!" said the raccoon, "that we did, my boy; and well have we kept the vow! And so long as Coon's tail has a single hair in it, will he ever cherish— Hello! what's that?" he cried with a sudden start, as a tiny brown creature darted swiftly across the path. "Woodmouse! I say, Woodmouse! stop a minute; you are just the fellow I want to see."

The woodmouse stopped and turned round, and greeted the two friends cordially.

"I have n't seen you for an age!" he said. "Coon, I supposed you had been asleep for a couple of months, at least. How does it happen that you are prowling about at this season?"

Coon briefly explained the state of the case, and then added : —

"I am specially glad to meet you, Wood-mouse, for I want to consult you about something. There are some mice in the cellar of the cottage, — brown mice. Very troublesome, thieving creatures they are, and we want to get rid of them. Now, I suppose they are relatives of yours, eh?"

"Ahem! well — yes," the woodmouse admitted reluctantly. "Distant, you know, quite distant; but — a — yes, they *are* relatives. A wretched, disreputable set, I have heard, though I never met any of them."

"You have heard quite correctly!" said the raccoon, warmly. "They are a great annoyance to the Madam, and to all of us. They almost take the food out of our mouths; they destroy things in the cellar, and — and in fact, we want to get rid of them."

The woodmouse stared at him in amazement. "Really, Mr. Coon," he said, laughing, "I should not have supposed, from my past acquaintance with you, that you would have any difficulty in getting rid of them."

Raccoons cannot blush, or our Coon certainly would have done so. He rubbed his nose helplessly, somewhat after the fashion of Bruin, and cast a half-comical, half-rueful glance at Toto. Finally he replied, —

"Well, you see, Woodmouse, things are rather different from usual this winter. The fact is, our Madam has a strong objection to — a — in point of fact, to slaughter; and she made it a condition of our coming to spend the winter with her, that we should not kill other creatures unless it were necessary. So I thought if we *could* get rid of those mice in any other way, it would please her. I suppose there is plenty of room in the forest for another family of mice?"

"Oh! as far as room goes," replied the woodmouse, "they have a range of ten miles in which to choose their home. I cannot promise to call on them, you know; that could not be expected. But if they behave themselves, they may in time overcome the prejudice against them."

"Very well," said Coon, "I shall send them, then. How are you all at home?" he added, "and what is going on in your set?"

Now it was the woodmouse's turn to look confused.

"My son is to be married on the second evening after this," he said. "That is the only thing I know of."

"What?" cried Coon. "Your son Prickear? Why, he is one of my best friends! How strange that I should have heard nothing of it!"

"We did n't know — we really thought — we supposed you were asleep!" stammered the woodmouse.

"And so you chose this time for the wedding?" said the raccoon. "Now, I call that unfriendly, Woodmouse, and I should n't have thought it of you."

The woodmouse stroked his whiskers, and looked piteously at his formidable acquaintance. "Don't be offended, Coon!" he said. "Perhaps — perhaps you will come to the wedding, after all. Eh? of course we should be delighted."

"Yes, to be sure I will come!" said the raccoon, cheerily. "*I* don't bear malice. Oh, yes! I will come, and Toto shall come, too. Where is it to take place?"

"We — we have engaged the cave for the evening," said the woodmouse, with some diffidence. "We have a large family connection, you know, and it is the only place big enough to hold them all."

Coon stared in amazement, and Toto gave a long whistle.

"The cave, eh?" he said. "I should say this was to be something very grand indeed. I should like very much to come, Woodmouse, if you think it would not trouble any of your family. I promise you that Coon shall be on his very best behavior, and — I'll tell you what!" he added, "I will provide the music, as I did last summer, at the Rabbit's Rinktum."

"No, not really! will you, though?" cried the little woodmouse, his slender tail quivering with delight. "We shall be infinitely obliged, Mr. Toto, infinitely obliged, sir! We shall count upon you both. Bring Cracker, too, and any other friends who may be staying with you. Would your grandmother, possibly — eh? care to come?"

"Thank you!" said Toto, gravely, "I think not. My grandmother never goes out in the evening."

"We might bring Bruin!" suggested Coon, with a sly wink at Toto.

But here the poor little woodmouse looked so unutterably distressed, that the two friends burst out laughing; and reassuring him by a word, bade him good-day, and proceeded on their walk.

CHAPTER V.

"AND now," said the squirrel, when the tea-things were cleared away that evening, "now for dancing-school. If we are going to a ball, we really must be more sure of our steps than we are now. Coon, oblige me with a whisk of your tail over the hearth. Some coals have fallen from the fire, and we shall be treading on them."

"When the coals are cold," replied the raccoon, "I shall be happy to oblige you. At present they are red-hot. And meantime, as I have no idea of dancing immediately after my supper, I will, if you like, tell you the story of the Useful Coal, which your request brings to my mind. It is short, and will not take much time from the dancing-lesson."

Right willingly the family all seated themselves around the blazing fire, and the raccoon began as follows: —

THE USEFUL COAL.

There was once a king whose name was Sligo. He was noted both for his riches and his kind heart. One evening, as he sat by his fireside, a coal fell out on the hearth. The King took up the tongs, intending to put it back on the fire, but the coal said: —

"If you will spare my life, and do as I tell you, I will save your treasure three times, and tell you the name of the thief who steals it."

These words gave the King great joy, for much treasure had been stolen from him of late, and none of his officers could discover the culprit. So he set the coal on the table, and said: —

"Pretty little black and red bird, tell me, what shall I do?"

"Put me in your waistcoat pocket," said the coal, "and take no more thought for to-night."

Accordingly the King put the coal in his pocket, and then, as he sat before the warm fire, he grew drowsy, and presently fell fast asleep.

When he had been asleep some time, the door opened, very softly, and the High Cel-larer peeped cautiously in. This was the one of the King's officers who had been most eager in searching for the thief. He now crept softly, softly, toward the King, and seeing that he was fast asleep, put his hand into his waistcoat-pocket; for in that waist-coat-pocket King Sligo kept the key of his treasure-chamber, and the High Cellarer was the thief. He put his hand into the waistcoat pocket. S-s-s-s-s! the coal burned it so fright-fully that he gave a loud shriek, and fell on his knees on the hearth.

"What is the matter?" cried the King, waking with a start.

"Alas! your Majesty," said the High Cel-larer, thrusting his burnt fingers into his bosom, that the King might not see them. "You were just on the point of falling forward into the fire, and I cried out, partly from fright and partly to waken you."

The King thanked the High Cellarer, and gave him a ruby ring as a reward. But when he was in his chamber, and making ready for bed, the coal said to him : —

"Once already have I saved your treasure, and to-night I shall save it again. Only put me on the table beside your bed, and you may sleep with a quiet heart."

So the King put the coal on the table, and himself into the bed, and was soon sound asleep. At midnight the door of the chamber opened very softly, and the High Cellarer peeped in again. He knew that at night King Sligo kept the key under his pillow, and he was coming to get it. He crept softly, softly, toward the bed, but as he drew near it, the coal cried out : —

"One eye sleeps, but the other eye wakes ! one eye sleeps, but the other eye wakes ! Who is this comes creeping, while honest men are sleeping ? "

The High Cellarer looked about him in

affright, and saw the coal burning fiery red in the darkness, and looking for all the world like a great flaming eye. In an agony of fear he fled from the chamber, crying, —

"Black and red! black and red!
The King has a devil to guard his bed."

And he spent the rest of the night shivering in the farthest garret he could find.

The next morning the coal said to the King : —

"Again this night have I saved your treasure, and mayhap your life as well. Yet a third time I shall do it, and this time you shall learn the name of the thief. But if I do this, you must promise me one thing, and that is that you will place me in your royal crown and wear me as a jewel. Will you do this?"

"That will I, right gladly!" replied King Sligo, "for a jewel indeed you are."

"That is well!" said the coal. "It is true that I am dying; but no matter. It is a fine thing to be a jewel in a king's crown, even if one is dead. Now listen, and follow my directions closely. As soon as I am quite black and dead, — which will be in about ten minutes from now, — you must take me in your hand and rub me all over and around the handle of the door of the treasure-chamber. A good part of me will be rubbed off, but there will be enough left to put in your crown. When you have thoroughly rubbed the door, lay the key of the treasure-chamber on your table, as if you had left it there by mistake. You may then go hunting or riding, but not for more than an hour; and when you return, you must instantly call all your court together, as if on business of the greatest importance. Invent some excuse for asking them to raise their hands, and then arrest the man whose hands are black. Do you understand ? "

" I do ! " replied King Sligo, fervently, " I do, and my warmest thanks, good Coal, are due to you for this — "

But here he stopped, for already the coal was quite black, and in less than ten minutes it was dead and cold. Then the King took it and rubbed it carefully over the door of the treasure-chamber, and laying the key of the door in plain sight on his dressing-table, he called his huntsmen together, and mounting his horse, rode away to the forest. As soon as he was gone, the High Cellarer, who had pleaded a headache when asked to join the hunt, crept softly to the King's room, and to his surprise found the key on the table. Full of joy, he sought the treasure-chamber at once, and began filling his pockets with gold and jewels, which he carried to his own apartment, returning greedily for more. In this way he opened and closed the door many times. Suddenly, as he was stooping over a silver barrel containing sapphires, he heard the sound of a trumpet, blown once, twice, thrice. The wicked thief started, for it was the signal for the entire court to appear instantly before the King, and the penalty of disobedience was death. Hastily cramming a handful of sapphires into his pocket, he stumbled to the door, which he closed and locked, putting the key also in his pocket, as there was no time to return it. He flew to the presence-chamber, where the lords of the kingdom were hastily assembling.

The King was seated on his throne, still in his hunting-dress, though he had put on his crown over his hat, which presented a peculiar appearance. It was with a majestic air, however, that he rose and said : —

" Nobles, and gentlemen of my court! I have called you together to pray for the soul of my lamented grandmother, who died, as you may remember, several years ago. In token of respect, I desire you all to raise your hands to Heaven."

The astonished courtiers, one and all, lifted their hands high in air. The King looked, and, behold! the hands of the High Cellarer were as black as soot! The King caused him to be arrested and searched, and the sapphires in his pocket, besides the key of the treasure-chamber, gave ample proof of his guilt. His head was removed at once, and the King had the useful coal, set in sapphires, placed in the

very front of his crown, where it was much
admired and praised as a BLACK DIAMOND.

"And *now*, Cracker, my boy," continued
the raccoon, rising from his seat by the fire,
"as you previously remarked, now for dancing-school!"

With these words he proceeded to sweep
the hearth carefully and gracefully with his
tail, while Toto and Bruin moved the chairs
and tables back against the wall. The grandmother's armchair was moved into the warm
chimney-corner, where she would be comfortably out of the way of the dancers; and
Pigeon Pretty perched on the old lady's
shoulder, "that the two sober-minded members of the family might keep each other in
countenance," she said. Toto ran into his
room, and returned with a little old fiddle
which had belonged to his grandfather, and
stationed himself at one end of the kitchen,
while the bear, the raccoon, and the squirrel
formed in line at the other.

"Now, then," said Master Toto, tapping

smartly on the fiddle. "Stand up straight, all of you! That's the first thing, you know."

Up they all went, — little Cracker sitting up jauntily, his tail cocked over his left ear, Coon pawing the air gracefully, but not quite sure of himself; while Bruin raised his huge form erect, and stood like a shaggy black giant, waiting further orders.

"Bow to partners!" cried Toto.

Coon and Cracker bowed to each other; and Bruin, having no partner, gravely saluted Miss Mary, who stood on one leg and surveyed the proceedings in silent but deep disdain.

"Jump, and change your feet!"

But this order, alas! was followed by dire confusion. Bruin dropped on all-fours, and frantically endeavored to stand on his fore-paws, with his hind-legs in the air, throwing up first one great shaggy leg and then another, and finally losing his balance and falling flat, with a thump that shook the whole house.

"Dear me!" cried the grandmother, starting from her chair. "Dear, dear me! Who is hurt? What has happened? Are any bones broken?"

"Oh, no! Madam," cried the bear, rising with surprising agility for one of his size; "it's nothing! nothing at all, I assure you. I — I was only jumping and changing my feet. But I cannot do it!" he added, in an aggrieved tone, to Toto. "It isn't possible, you know, for a fellow of my build to — a — do that sort of thing. You shouldn't, really — "

"Oh, Bruin! Bruin!" cried Toto, wiping the tears from his eyes, as he leaned against the dresser in a paroxysm of merriment. "I didn't *mean* you to do that! Look here! this is the way. You jump — *so!* and change your feet — *so!* as you come down. There, look at Coon; he has the idea, perfectly!"

The astute Coon, in truth, seeing Bruin's error, had stood quietly in his place till he saw Toto perform the mystic manœuvre of "jump and change feet," and had then begun to practise it with a quiet grace and ease, as if he had done it all his life.

" Now, then, attention all !   Forward and back ! "   And he played a lively air on his fiddle. — PAGE 97.

The squirrel, meanwhile, had obeyed the first part of the order by jumping to the top of the clock, where he sat inspecting his little black feet with an air of comical perplexity.

"Change them, eh?" he said. "What's the matter with them? They'll do very well yet awhile."

"Don't be absurd, Cracker!" said Toto, rather severely. "Come down and take your place at once! Now, then, attention all! Forward and back!" and he played a lively air on his fiddle.

The bear brightened up at once. "Ah!" he said, "I am all right when we come to forward and back. Tum-tiddy tum-tum, tum-tum-tum!" and he pranced forward, put out one foot, and slid back again, with an air of enjoyment that was pleasant to behold.

"That's right!" said the master, approvingly. "Stand a little straighter, Bruin! Cracker, you don't point your toe enough. Hold your head up, Coon, and don't be looking round at your tail every minute. *Tum*-tiddy tum-tum, *tum*-tum-tum! *tiddy*-iddy tum-

tum, *tum*-tum-tum! Balance to partners! Here, Bruin! you can balance to me. Turn partners, and back to places! There, now you may rest a moment before you begin on the waltz step."

"Ah! that is *my* delight," said the squirrel. "What a sensation we shall make at the wedding! One of the woodmouse's daughters is very pretty, with such a nice little nose, and such bright eyes! I shall ask her to waltz with me."

"There won't be any one of my size there, I suppose," said the raccoon. "You and I will have to be partners, Toto."

"And I must stay at home and waltz alone!" said Bruin, goodnaturedly. "It is a misfortune, in some ways, to be so big."

"But great good fortune in others, Bruin, dear!" said Pigeon Pretty, affectionately. "I, for one, would not have you smaller, for the world!"

"Nor would I!" said the grandmother, heartily. "Bruin, my friend and protector, your size and strength are the greatest possible comfort to me, coupled as they are with a kind heart and a willing —"

"Paw!" cried Toto. "Your sentiments are most correct, Granny, dear; but Bruin *must* not stand bowing in the middle of the room, even if he is grateful. Go in the corner, Bruin, and practise your steps, while I take a turn with Coon. And you, Cracker, can —"

But Master Cracker did not wait for instructions. He had been watching the parrot for some minutes, with his head on one side and his eyes twinkling with merriment; and now, springing suddenly upon her perch, he caught the astonished bird round the body, leaped with her to the floor, and began to whirl her round the room at a surprising rate, in tolerably good time to the lively waltz that Toto was whistling. Miss Mary gasped for breath, and fluttered her wings wildly, trying to escape from her tormentor, and presently, finding her voice, she shrieked aloud : —

"Ke-ke-kee! ki-ko! ki-ko-KAA! Let me go,

you little wretch! Let me go this instant, or
I 'll peck your eyes out! I will—"

"Oh, no, you won't, my dear!" said Cracker. "You would n't have the heart to do
that; for then how could I look at you, the
delight of my life? Tiddy-*tum*! tiddy-*tum*!
tiddy-*tum* tum-tum! just see what a pretty
step it is! You will enjoy it immensely, as
soon as you know it a little better." And
he whirled her round faster and faster, trying
to keep pace with Coon and Toto, who were
circling in graceful curves.

Suddenly the grandmother uttered an ex-
clamation. "Toto!" she cried, "did you
put that custard pie out in the snow to cool?
Bruin does n't like it hot, you know."

Toto, his head still dizzy from waltzing,
looked about him in bewilderment.

"Did I?" he said. "I am sure I don't
know! I don't remember what I did with it.
Oh, yes, I do, though!" he added hastily.
"It is there, on that chair. Bruin! Bruin, I
say! mind what you are about. It is just
behind you."

Thus adjured, the good bear, who had been gravely revolving by himself in the corner until he was quite blind, tried to stop short; at the same instant the squirrel and the parrot, stumbling against his shaggy paw, fell over it in a confused heap of feathers and fur. He stepped hastily back to avoid treading on them, lost his balance, and sat down heavily — on the custard pie!

At the crash of the platter, the squirrel released Miss Mary, who flew screaming to her perch; the grandmother wrung her hands and lamented, begging to be told what had happened, and who was hurt; and the unfortunate Bruin, staggering to his feet, stared aghast at the ruin he had wrought. It was a very complete ruin, certainly, for the platter was in small fragments, while most of its contents were clinging to his own shaggy black coat.

"Well, old fellow," said Toto, "you have done it now, have n't you? I tried to stop you, but I was too late."

"Yes," replied the bear, solemnly, "I have

done it now!   And I have also done *with* it now.   Dear Madam," he added, turning to the old lady, " please forgive me ! I have spoiled your pie, and broken your platter; but I have also learned a lesson, which I ought to have learned before, — that is, that waltzing is not my forte, and that, as the old saying is, 'A bullfrog cannot dance in a grasshopper's nest.' This is my last dancing lesson!"

CHAPTER VI.

IT was a bright clear night, when Toto, accompanied by the raccoon and the squirrel, started from home to attend the wedding of the woodmouse's eldest son. The moon was shining gloriously, and her bright cold rays turned everything they touched to silver. The long icicles hanging from the eaves of the cottage glittered like crystal spears; the snow sparkled as if diamond-dust were strewn over its powdery surface. The raccoon shook himself as he walked along, and looked about him with his keen bright eyes.

"What a fine night this would be for a hunt!" he said, sniffing the cold bracing air eagerly. "I smell something, surely! What is it?"

"Rats, maybe!" suggested the squirrel. "There is the track of one yonder."

"No, this is not a rat!" said the raccoon, sniffing again. "It's a — it's a cat! that's what it is, a cat! Do you see a track anywhere? I wonder how a cat came here, anyhow. I should like to chase her! It is a long time since I chased a cat."

"Oh, never mind the cat now, Coon!" cried Toto. "We are late for the wedding as it is, with all your prinking. Besides," he added slyly, "I did n't lend you that red cravat to chase cats in."

The raccoon instantly threw off his professional eagerness, and resumed the air of complacent dignity with which he had begun the walk. Never before had he been so fully impressed with the sense of his own charms. The red ribbon which he had begged from Toto set off his dark fur and bright eyes to perfection; and he certainly was a very handsome fellow, as he frisked daintily along, his tail curling gracefully over his back.

"We shall make a sensation!" he said cheerfully; "we shall certainly make a sensation. Don't you think so, Toto?"

"I do, indeed," replied Toto; "though it is a great pity that you and Cracker did n't let me put your tails in curl-papers last night, as I offered to do. You can't think what an improvement it would have been."

"The cow offered to lend me her bell," said Cracker, "to wear round my neck, but it was too big, you know. She's the dearest old thing, that cow! I had a grand game, this morning, jumping over her back and balancing myself on her horns. Why doesn't she live in the house, with the rest of us?"

"Oh!" said Toto, "one *couldn't* have a cow in the house. She's too big, in the first place; and besides, Granny would not like it. One could not make a companion of a cow! I don't know exactly why, but that sort of animal is entirely different from you wood-creatures."

"The difference is, my dear," said the raccoon, loftily, "that we have been accustomed to good society, and know something of its laws; while persons like Mrs. Cow are absolutely ignorant of such matters. Abso-

lutely ignorant!" he repeated, impressively.
"Why, only yesterday I went out to the
barn, and being in need of a little exercise,
thought I would amuse myself by swinging
on her tail. And the creature, instead of
saying, 'Mr. Coon, I am sensible of the
honor you bestow upon me, but your well-
proportioned figure is perhaps heavier than
you are aware of,' or something of that sort,
just kicked me off, without saying a word.
Kicked, Toto! I give you my word for it.
Kicked *me!*"

"Humph!" said the squirrel, "I think I
should have done the same in her place.
But see, here we are at the cave. Just look
at the tracks in the snow! Why, there must
be a thousand persons here, at least."

Indeed, the snow was covered in every direction with the prints of little feet, — feet
that had hopped, had run, had crept from
all sides of the forest, and had met in front
of this low opening, from which the brambles
and creeping vines had been carefully cleared
away. Torches of light-wood were blazing

on either side, lighting up the gloomy entrance for several feet, and from within came a confused murmur of many voices, as of hundreds of small creatures squeaking, piping, and chattering in every variety of tone.

"We are late!" said Coon. "Everybody is here. So much the better; we shall make all the more sensation. Toto, is my neck-tie straight?"

"Quite straight," replied Toto. "You look like — like — "

"Like a popinjay!" muttered the squirrel, who had no neck-tie. "Come along, will you, Coon?" And the three companions entered the cave together.

A brilliant scene it was that presented itself before their eyes. The cave was lighted not only by glow-worms, but by light-wood torches stuck in every available crack and cranny of the walls. The floor was sprinkled with fine white sand, clean and glittering, while branches of holly and alder placed in the corners added still more to the general air of festivity. As to the guests,

they were evidently enjoying themselves
greatly, to judge from the noise they were
making. There were a great many of them,
— hundreds, or perhaps even thousands,
though it was impossible to count them,
as they were constantly moving, hopping,
leaping, jumping, creeping, trotting, running, even flying. Never were so many
tiny creatures seen together. There were
woodmice, of course, by the hundred, — old
and young, big and little; cousins, uncles,
aunts, grandmothers, of the bride and bridegroom. There were respectable field-mice,
looking like well-to-do farmers, as indeed they
were; frisky kangaroo-mice, leaping about
on their long hind-legs, to the admiration of
all those whose legs were short. There were
all the moles, of both families, — those who
wore plain black velvet without any ornament, and those who had lovely rose-colored
stars at the end of their noses. These last
gentlemen were very aristocratic indeed, and
the woodmice felt highly honored by their
presence. Besides all these, the squirrels

had been invited, and had come in full force, the Grays and the Reds and the Chipmunks; and Mr. and Mrs. Titmouse were there, and old Mrs. Shrew and her daughters, and I don't know how many more. Hundreds and hundreds of guests, none of them bigger than a squirrel, and most of them much smaller.

You can perhaps imagine the effect that was produced on this gay assembly by the sudden appearance among them of a RACCOON and a BOY! There was a confused murmur for a moment, a quick affrighted glance, and then dead silence. Not a creature dared to move; not a tail waved, not a whisker quivered; all the tiny creatures stood as if turned to stone, gazing in mute terror and supplication at their formidable visitors. The bride, who had just entered from a side-cave on her father's arm, prepared to faint; the bridegroom threw his arms about her and glared fiercely at the intruders, his tiny heart swelling as high as if he were a lion instead of a very small red mouse. Mr. Woodmouse, Senior, alone retained his presence of mind. He hastened to greet his formidable guests, and bade them welcome in a voice which, though tremulous, tried hard to be cordial.

"Mr. Coon," he said, "you are welcome, most welcome. Mr. Toto, your most obedient, sir. Cracker, I am delighted to see you. Very good of you all, I'm sure, to honor this little occasion with your distinguished presence. Will you — ah! — hum — will you sit down?"

The little host hesitated over this invitation; it would not be polite to ask his guests to be careful lest they should sit down *on* the other guests, and yet they were so *very* large, and took up so *much* room, — two of them, at least! Coon, delighted at the sensation he had produced, was as gracious as possible, and sitting down with great care so as to avoid any catastrophe, looked about him with so benign an expression that the rest of the company began to take heart, and whiskers were pricked and tails were cocked again.

"This is delightful, Mr. Woodmouse!" he said heartily, — "this is really delightful! A brilliant occasion, indeed! But I do not see your son, the happy — Ah! there he is. Prick-ear, you rascal, come here! Are you too proud to speak to your old friends?"

Thus adjured, the young woodmouse left his bride in her mother's care and came forward, looking half pleased and half angry. "Good evening, Coon!" he said. "I was not sure whether you *were* a friend, after our last meeting. But I am very glad to see you, and I bear no malice."

And with this he shook paws with an air of magnanimity. Coon rubbed his nose, as he was apt to do when a little confused.

"Oh! ah! to be sure!" he said. "I had quite forgotten that little matter. But say no more about it, my boy; say no more about it! By-gones are by-gones, and we should think of nothing but pleasure on an occasion like the present." With a graceful and condescending wave of his paw he dismissed the past, and continued: "Pray, introduce me to your charming bride! I assure you I am positively longing to make her acquaintance. After you, my boy; after you!" and he crossed the room and joined the bridal party.

"What trouble did your son have with Coon?" Toto inquired of Mr. Woodmouse. "Nothing serious, I trust?"

"Why — ah! — well!" said his host, in some embarrassment, "it came *near* being serious, — at least Prick-ear thought it did. It seems he met Mr. Coon one day last autumn, when he was bringing home a load of checkerberries for supper. Mr. Coon wanted the checkerberries, and — ah! — in point of fact, ate them; and when Prick-ear remonstrated, he chased him all round the forest, vowing that if he caught him he would — if you will excuse my mentioning such a thing — eat *him* too. Now, that sort of thing is very painful, Mr. Toto; very painful indeed it is, I assure you, sir. And though Prick-ear escaped by running into a mole's burrow, I must confess that he has *not* felt kindly toward Mr. Coon since then."

"Very natural," said Toto, gravely. "I don't wonder at it."

"It *has* occurred to me," continued the woodmouse, "that possibly it may have been only a joke on Mr. Coon's part. Eh? what do you think? Seeing him so friendly and condescending here to-night, one can hardly suppose that he *really* — eh? — could have intended —"

"He certainly would not do such a thing *now*," said Toto, decidedly, "certainly not. He has the kindest feeling for all your family."

"A — exactly! exactly!" cried the woodmouse, highly delighted. "Most gratifying, I'm sure. But I see that the ceremony is about to begin. If you *would* excuse me, Mr. Toto —"

And the little host bowed himself away, leaving Toto to seat himself at leisure and watch the proceedings. These were certainly very interesting. The bride, an extremely pretty little mouse, was attired in a very becoming travelling-dress of brown fur, which fitted her to perfection. The ceremony was performed by a star-nosed mole of high distinction, who delivered a learned and impressive discourse to the young couple, and ended by presenting them with three leaves of wintergreen, of which one was eaten by each separately, while they nibbled the third together, in token of their united lives. When they met in the middle of the leaf, they rubbed noses together, and the ceremony was finished.

Then everybody advanced to rub noses with the bride, and to shake paws with the happy bridegroom. One of the first to do so was the raccoon, who comported himself with a grace and dignity which attracted the admiration of all. The little bride was nearly frightened to death, it is true; but she bore up bravely, for her husband whispered in her ear that Mr. Coon was one of his dearest friends, *now*.

Meanwhile, no one was enjoying the festivity more thoroughly than our little friend Cracker. He was whisking and frisking about from one group to another, greeting old friends, making new acquaintances, hearing all the wood-gossip of the winter, and telling in return of the wonderful life that he and Bruin and Coon were leading. His own relations were most deeply interested in all he had to tell; but while his cousins were loud in their expressions of delight and of envy, some of the elders shook their heads. Uncle Munkle, a sedate and portly chipmunk, looked very grave as he heard of all the doings at the cottage, and presently he beckoned Cracker to one side, and addressed him in a low tone.

"Cracker, my boy," he said, "I don't quite like all this, do you know? Toto and his grandmother are all very well, though they seem to have a barbarous way of living; but who is this Mrs. Cow, about whom you have so much to say; not a domestic animal, I trust?"

"Why — yes!" Cracker admitted, rather

reluctantly, " she *is* a domestic animal, Uncle ; but she is a very good one, I assure you, and not objectionable in any way."

The old chipmunk looked deeply offended. "I did not expect this of you, Cracker!" he said severely, "I did not, indeed. This is the first time, to my knowledge, that a member of my family has had anything to do with a domestic animal. I am disappointed in you, sir ; distinctly disappointed!"

There was a pause, in which the delinquent Cracker found nothing to say, and then his uncle added : —

"And in what condition are your teeth, pray ? I suppose you are letting them grow, while you eat those wretched messes of soft food. Have you *any* proper food, at all ?"

" Oh, yes ! " exclaimed Cracker. " Indeed, Uncle Munkle, my teeth are in excellent condition. Just look at them !" and he exhibited two shining rows of teeth as sharp as those of a newly-set saw. " We have plenty of nuts ; more than I ever had before, I assure you. Toto got quantities of them in the autumn, on purpose for me; and there are great heaps of hazels and beech-nuts and hickories piled up in the barn-chamber, where I can go and help myself when I please. And almonds, too!" he added. "Oh, they are *so* jolly!"

Uncle Munkle looked mollified; he even seemed interested.

"Almonds?" he said. "They are foreign nuts, and don't grow in this part of the world. I tasted some once. Where did Toto get them, do you think?"

"He bought them of a pedler," said Cracker. "I know he would give you some, Uncle, if you asked him. Why won't you come out and see us, some day?"

At this moment a loud and lively whistle was heard,—first three notes of warning, and then Toto's merriest jig,—which put all serious thoughts to flight, and set the whole company dancing. Cracker flew across the room to a charming young red squirrel on whom he had had his eye for some time, made his bow, and was soon showing off to her admiring gaze the fine steps which he had learned in the kitchen at home. The woodmice skipped and hopped merrily about; the kangaroo-mice danced with long, graceful bounds,—three short hops after each one. It is easy to do when you know just how. As for the moles, they ran round and round in a circle, with their noses to the ground, and thought very well of themselves.

Presently Toto changed his tune from a jig to a waltz; and then he and Coon danced together, to the admiration of all beholders. Round they went, and round and round, circling in graceful curves,—Toto never pausing in his whistle, Coon's scarlet necktie waving like a banner in the breeze.

"Yes, that is a sight worth seeing!" said a woodmouse to a mole. "It is a pity, just for this once, that you have not eyes to see it."

"Are their coats of black velvet?" inquired the mole. "And have they stars on their noses? Tell me that."

"No," replied the woodmouse.

"I thought as much!" said the mole, contemptuously. "Vulgar people, probably. I

have no desire to *see* them, as you call it. Are
we to have anything to eat?" he added.
"That is of more consequence, to my mind.
One can show one's skill in dancing, but that
does not fill the stomach, and mine warns me
that it is empty."

At this very moment the music stopped,
and the voice of the host was heard announ-
cing that supper was served in the side-cave.
The mole waited to hear no more, but rushed
as fast as his legs would carry him, following
his unerring nose in the direction where the
food lay. Bolting into the supper-room,
he ran violently against a neatly arranged
pyramid of hazel-nuts, and down it came, rat-
tling and tumbling over the greedy mole, and
finally burying him completely. The rest of
the company coming soberly in, each gentleman with his partner, saw the heaving and
quaking mountain of nuts beneath which the
mole was struggling, and he was rescued amid
much laughter and merriment.

That was a supper indeed! There were
nuts of all kinds, — butternuts, chestnuts,

beech-nuts, hickories, and hazels.   There were huge piles of acorns, of several kinds, — the long slender brown-satin ones, and the fat red-and-brown ones, with a woolly down on them. There were partridge-berries and checker-berries, and piles of fragrant, spicy leaves of wintergreen.   And there was sassafras-bark and spruce-gum, and a great dish of golden corn, — a present from the field-cousins. Really, it gives one an appetite only to think of it!   And I verily believe that there never was such a nibbling, such a gnawing, such a champing and cracking and throwing away of shells, since first the forest was a forest. When the guests were thirsty, there was root-beer, served in birch-bark goblets; and when one had drunk all the beer one ate the goblet; which was very pleasant, and more-over saved some washing of dishes.   And so all were very merry, and the star-nosed moles ate so much that their stars turned purple, and they had to be led home by their field-mouse neighbors.

At the close of the feast, the bride and

groom departed for their own home, which was charmingly fitted up under an elder-bush, from the berries of which they could make their own wine. " Such a convenience!" said all the family. And finally, after a last wild dance, the company separated, the lights were put out, and " the event of the season " was over.

CHAPTER VII.

TOTO and his companions walked homeward in high spirits. The air was crisp
and tingling; the snow crackled merrily beneath their feet; and though the moon had
set, the whole sky was ablaze with stars,
sparkling with the keen, winter radiance
which one sees only in cold weather.

"Pretty wedding, eh, Toto?" said the
raccoon.

"Very pretty," said Toto; "very pretty
indeed. I have enjoyed myself immensely.
What good people they are, those little woodmice. See here! they made me fill all my
pockets with checkerberries and nuts for the
others at home, and they sent so many mes-
sages of regret and apology to Bruin that I
shall not get any of them straight."

"Hello!" said the squirrel, who had been
gazing up into the sky, "what's that?"

"What's *what?*" asked the raccoon.

"*That!*" repeated Cracker. "That big thing with a tail, up among the stars."

His companions both stared upward in their turn, and Toto exclaimed,—

"Why, it's a comet! I never saw one before, but I know what they look like, from the pictures. It certainly *is* a comet!"

"And *what*, if I may be so bold as to ask," said Coon, "*is* a comet?"

"Why, it's — it's — THAT, you know!" said Toto.

"Exactly!" said Coon. "What a clear way you have of putting things, to be sure!"

"Well," cried Toto, laughing, "I'm afraid I cannot put it *very* clearly, because I don't know just *exactly* what comets are, myself. But they are heavenly bodies, and they come and go in the sky, with tails; and sometimes you don't see one again for a thousand years; and though you don't see them move, they are really going like lightning all the time."

Coon and Cracker looked at each other, as if they feared that their companion was losing his wits.

"Have they four legs?" asked Cracker. "And what do they live on?"

"They have no legs," replied Toto, "nothing but heads and tails; and I don't believe they live on anything, unless," he added, with a twinkle in his eye, "they get milk from the milky way."

The raccoon looked hard at Toto, and then equally hard at the comet, which for its part spread its shining tail among the constellations, and took no notice whatever of him.

"Can't you give us a little more of this precious information?" he said with a sneer. "It is so valuable, you know, and we are so likely to believe it, Cracker and I, being two greenhorns, as you seem to think."

Toto flushed, and his brow clouded for an instant, for Coon could be so *very* disagreeable when he tried; but the next moment he threw back his head and laughed merrily.

"Yes, I will!" he cried. "I *will* give you

more information, old fellow. I will tell you a story I once heard about a comet. It is n't true, you know, but what of that? You will believe it just as much as you would the truth. Listen, now, both you cross fellows, to the story of

THE NAUGHTY COMET.

The door of the Comet House was open. In the great court-yard stood hundreds of comets, of all sizes and shapes. Some were puffing and blowing, and arranging their tails, all ready to start; others had just come in, and looked shabby and forlorn after their long journeyings, their tails drooping disconsolately; while others still were switched off on side-tracks, where the tinker and the tailor were attending to their wants, and setting them to rights. In the midst of all stood the Comet Master, with his hands behind him, holding a very long stick with a very sharp point. The comets knew just how the point of that stick felt, for they were prodded with it whenever they misbehaved themselves;

accordingly, they all remained very quiet, while he gave his orders for the day.

In a distant corner of the court-yard lay an old comet, with his tail comfortably curled up around him.   He was too old to go out, so he enjoyed himself at home in a quiet way. Beside him stood a very young comet, with a very short tail.   He was quivering with excitement, and occasionally cast sharp impatient glances at the Comet Master.

"Will he *never* call me?" he exclaimed, but in an undertone, so that only his companion could hear.   "He knows I am dying to go out, and for that very reason he pays no attention to me.   I dare not leave my place, for you know what he is."

"Ah!" said the old comet, slowly, "if you had been out as often as I have, you would not be in such a hurry.   Hot, tiresome work, *I* call it.   And what does it all amount to?"

"Ay, that's the point!" exclaimed the young comet.   "What *does* it all amount to?   That is what I am determined to find out.   I cannot understand your going on, travelling and travelling, and never finding out why you do it. *I* shall find out, you may be very sure, before I have finished my first journey."

"Better not! better not!" answered the old comet. "You'll only get into trouble. Nobody knows except the Comet Master and the Sun. The Master would cut you up into inch pieces if you asked him, and the Sun —"

"Well, what about the Sun?" asked the young comet, eagerly.

"Short-tailed Comet No. 73!" rang suddenly, clear and sharp, through the court-yard.

The young comet started as if he had been shot, and in three bounds he stood before the Comet Master, who looked fixedly at him.

"You have never been out before," said the Master.

"No, sir!" replied No. 73; and he knew better than to add another word.

"You will go out now," said the Comet Master. "You will travel for thirteen weeks and three days, and will then return. You will avoid the neighborhood of the Sun, the

Earth, and the planet Bungo. You will turn to the left on meeting other comets, and you are not allowed to speak to meteors. These are your orders. Go!"

At the word, the comet shot out of the gate and off into space, his short tail bobbing as he went.

Ah! here was something worth living for. No longer shut up in that tiresome court-yard, waiting for one's tail to grow, but out in the free, open, boundless realm of space, with leave to shoot about here and there and everywhere — well, *nearly* everywhere — for thirteen whole weeks! Ah, what a glorious prospect! How swiftly he moved! How well his tail looked, even though it was still rather short! What a fine fellow he was, altogether!

For two or three weeks our comet was the happiest creature in all space; too happy to think of anything except the joy of frisking about. But by-and-by he began to wonder about things, and that is always dangerous for a comet.

"I wonder, now," he said, "why I may not go near the planet Bungo. I have always heard that he was the most interesting of all the planets. And the Sun! how I *should* like to know a little more about the Sun! And, by the way, that reminds me that all this time I have never found out *why* I am travelling. It shows how I have been enjoying myself, that I have forgotten it so long; but now I must certainly make a point of finding out. Hello! there comes Long-Tail No. 45. I mean to ask him."

So he turned out to the left, and waited till No. 45 came along. The latter was a middle-aged comet, very large, and with an uncommonly long tail, — quite preposterously long, our little No. 73 thought, as he shook his own tail and tried to make as much of it as possible.

"Good morning, Mr. Long-Tail!" he said as soon as the other was within speaking distance. "Would you be so very good as to tell me what you are travelling for?"

"For six months," answered No. 45 with a

puff and a snort. "Started a month ago; five months still to go."

"Oh, I don't mean that!" exclaimed Short-Tail No. 73. "I mean *why* are you travelling at all?"

"Comet Master sent me!" replied No. 45, briefly.

"But what for?" persisted the little comet. "What is it all about? What good does it do? *Why* do we travel for weeks and months and years? That's what I want to find out."

"Don't know, I'm sure!" said the elder, still more shortly. "What's more, don't care!"

The little comet fairly shook with amazement and indignation. "You don't care!" he cried. "Is it possible? And how long, may I ask, have you been travelling hither and thither through space, without knowing or caring why?"

"Long enough to learn not to ask stupid questions!" answered Long-Tail No. 45. "Good morning to you!"

And without another word he was off, with his preposterously long tail spreading itself like a luminous fan behind him. The little comet looked after him for some time in silence. At last he said: —

"Well, *I* call that simply *disgusting!* An ignorant, narrow-minded old —"

"Hello, cousin!" called a clear merry voice just behind him. "How goes it with you? Shall we travel together? Our roads seem to go in the same direction."

The comet turned and saw a bright and sparkling meteor. "I — I — must not speak to you!" said No. 73, confusedly.

"Not speak to me!" exclaimed the meteor, laughing. "Why, what's the matter? What have I done? I never saw you before in my life."

"N-nothing that I know of," answered No. 73, still more confused.

"Then why must n't you speak to me?" persisted the meteor, giving a little skip and jump. "Eh? tell me that, will you? *Why* must n't you?"

"I — don't — know!" answered the little comet, slowly, for he was ashamed to say boldly, as he ought to have done, that it was against the orders of the Comet Master.

"Oh, gammon!" cried the meteor, with another skip. "*I* know! Comet Master, eh? But a fine high-spirited young fellow like you is n't going to be afraid of that old tyrant. Come along, I say! If there were any *real reason* why you should not speak to me —"

"That's just what I say," interrupted the comet, eagerly. "What is the reason? Why don't they tell it to me?"

"'Cause there is n't any!" rejoined the meteor. "Come along!"

After a little more hesitation, the comet yielded, and the two frisked merrily along, side by side. As they went, No. 73 confided all his vexations to his new friend, who sympathized warmly with him, and spoke in most disrespectful terms of the Comet Master.

"A pretty sort of person to dictate to you, when he has n't the smallest sign of a tail himself! I would n't submit to it!" cried the meteor. "As to the other orders, some of them are not so bad. Of course, nobody would want to go near that stupid, poky Earth, if he could possibly help it; and the planet Bungo is — ah — is not a very nice planet, I believe. [The fact is, the planet Bungo contains a large reform-school for unruly meteors, but our friend made no mention of that.] But as for the Sun, — the bright, jolly, delightful Sun, — why, I am going to take a nearer look at him myself. Come on! We will go together, in spite of the Comet Master."

Again the little comet hesitated and demurred; but after all, he had already broken one rule, and why not another? He would be punished in any case, and he might as well get all the pleasure he could. Reasoning thus, he yielded once more to the persuasions of the meteor, and together they shot through the great space-world, taking their way straight toward the Sun.

When the Sun saw them coming, he smiled and seemed much pleased. He stirred his fire, and shook his shining locks, and blazed brighter and brighter, hotter and hotter. The heat seemed to have a strange effect on the comet, for he began to go faster and faster.

"Hold on!" said the meteor. "Why are you hurrying so? I cannot keep up with you."

"I cannot stop myself!" cried No. 73. "Something is drawing me forward, faster and faster!"

On he went at a terrible rate, the meteor following as best he might. Several planets which he passed shouted to him in warning tones, but he could not hear what they said. The Sun stirred his fire again, and blazed brighter and brighter, hotter and hotter; and forward rushed the wretched little comet, faster and faster, faster and faster!

"Catch hold of my tail and stop me!" he shrieked to the meteor. "I am shrivelling, burning up, in this fearful heat! Stop me, for pity's sake!"

But the meteor was already far behind,

and had stopped short to watch his companion's headlong progress. And now,— ah, me!— now the Sun opened his huge fiery mouth. The comet made one desperate effort to stop himself, but it was in vain. An awful, headlong plunge through the intervening space; a hissing and crackling; a shriek,— and the fiery jaws had closed on Short-Tail No. 73, forever!

"Dear me!" said the meteor. "How very shocking! I quite forgot that the Sun ate comets. I must be off, or I shall get an æon in the Reform School for this. I am really very sorry, for he was a nice little comet!"

And away frisked the meteor, and soon forgot all about it.

But in the great court-yard in front of the Comet House, the Master took a piece of chalk, and crossed out No. 73 from the list of short-tailed comets on the slate that hangs on the door. Then he called out, "No. 1 Express, come forward!" and the swiftest of all the comets stood before him, brilliant and beautiful, with a bewildering magnificence of tail. The Comet Master spoke sharply and decidedly, as usual, but not unkindly.

"No. 73, Short-Tail," he said, "has disobeyed orders, and has in consequence been devoured by the Sun."

Here there was a great sensation among the comets.

"No. 1," continued the Master, "you will start immediately, and travel until you find a runaway meteor, with a red face and blue hair. You are permitted to make inquiries of respectable bodies, such as planets or satellites. When found, you will arrest him and take him to the planet Bungo. My compliments to the Meteor Keeper, and I shall be obliged if he will give this meteor two æons in the Reform School. I trust," he continued, turning to the assembled comets, "that this will be a lesson to all of you!"

And I believe it was.

CHAPTER VIII.

" BRUIN, what do you think? Oh, Bruin! what *do* you think?" Thus spoke the little squirrel as he sat perch'ed on his big friend's shoulder, the day after the wedding party.

"What do I think?" repeated the bear. "Why, I think that you are tickling my ear, Master Cracker, and that if you do not stop, I shall be under the painful necessity of knocking you off on the floor."

"Oh, that is n't the kind of thinking I mean!" replied Cracker, impudently flirting the tip of his tail into the good bear's eye. "*That* is of no consequence, you great big fellow! What are your ears for, if not for me to tickle? I mean, what do you think I heard at the party, last night?"

"A great deal of nonsense!" replied the bear, promptly.

"Bruin, I shall certainly be obliged to shake you!" cried the squirrel. "I shall shake you till your teeth rattle, if you give me any more of this impudence. So behave yourself now, and listen to me. I was talking with Chipper last night, — my cousin, you know, who lives at the other end of the wood, — and he told me something that really quite troubled me. You remember old Baldhead?"

"Well, yes!" said Bruin, "I should say I did. He hasn't been in our part of the wood again, has he?"

"Oh, no!" replied Cracker. "He is not likely to go anywhere for a long time, I should say. He has broken his leg, Chipper tells me, and has been shut up in his cavern for a week and more."

"Dear me!" said the kind-hearted bear. "I am very sorry to hear it! How does the poor old man get his food?"

"Chipper didn't seem to think he *could* get any," replied the squirrel. "He peeped in at the door, yesterday, and saw him lying in his bunk, looking very pale and thin. He tried once or twice to get up, but fell back again; and Chipper is sure there was nothing to eat in the cave. I thought I would n't say anything to Coon or Toto last night, but would wait till I had told you."

"It must be seen to at once!" cried Bruin, starting up. "I will go myself, and take care of the poor man till his leg is well. Where are the Madam and Toto? We must tell them at once."

The blind grandmother was in the kitchen, rolling out pie-crust. She listened, with exclamations of pity and concern, to Cracker's account of the poor old hermit, and agreed with Bruin that aid must be sent to him without delay. "I will pack a basket at once," she said, "with nourishing food, bandages for the broken leg, and some simple medicines; and Toto, you will take it to the poor man, will you not, dear?"

"Of course I will!" said Toto, heartily.

But Bruin said: "No, dear Madam! I will go myself. Our Toto's heart is big, but he is not strong enough to take care of a sick person. It is surely best for me to go."

The grandmother hesitated. "Dear Bruin," she said, "of course you *would* be the best nurse on many accounts; but if the man is weak and nervous, I am afraid — you alarmed him once, you know, and possibly the sight of you, coming in suddenly, might — "

"Speak out, Granny!" cried Toto, laughing. "You think Bruin would simply frighten the man to death, or at best into a fit; and you are quite right. I'll tell you what, old fellow!" he added, turning to Bruin, who looked sadly crestfallen at this throwing of cold water on the fire of his kindly intentions, "we will go together, and then the whole thing will be easily managed. I will go in first, and tell the hermit all about you; and then, when his mind is prepared, you can come in and make him comfortable."

The good bear brightened up at this, and gladly assented to Toto's proposition; and the two set out shortly after, Bruin carrying a large basket of food, and Toto a small

one containing medicines and bandages. Part
of the food was for their own lunch, as they
had a long walk before them, and would not
be back till long past dinner-time. They
trudged briskly along, — Toto whistling merrily as usual, but his companion very grave
and silent.

"What ails you, old fellow?" asked the
boy, when a couple of miles had been traversed in this manner. "Has our account of
the wedding made you pine with envy, and
wish yourself a mouse?"

"No!" replied the bear, slowly, "oh, no!
I should not like to be a mouse, or anything
of that sort. But I do wish, Toto, that I was
not so frightfully ugly!"

"Ugly!" cried Toto, indignantly, "who
said you were ugly? What put such an idea
into your head?"

"Why, you yourself," said the bear, sadly.
"You said I would frighten the man to death,
or into a fit. Now, one must be horribly ugly
to do that, you know."

"My *dear* Bruin," cried Toto, "it isn't

because you are *ugly*; why, you are a perfect beauty — for a bear. But — well — you are *very* large, you know, and somewhat shaggy, if you don't mind my saying so; and you must remember that most bears are very savage, disagreeable creatures. How is anybody who sees you for the first time to know that you are the best and dearest old fellow in the world? Besides," he added, "have you forgotten how you frightened this very hermit when he stole your honey, last year?"

Bruin hung his head, and looked very sheepish. "I should n't roar, now, of course," he said. "I meant to be very gentle, and just put one paw in, and then the end of my nose, and so get into the cave by degrees, you know."

Toto had his doubts as to the soothing effect which would have been produced by this singular measure, but he had not the heart to say so; and after a pause, Bruin continued : —

" Of course, however, you and Madam were quite right, — quite right you were, my boy. But I was wondering, just now, whether there were not some way of making myself less frightful. Now, you and Madam have no hair on your faces, — none anywhere, in fact, except a very little on the top of your head. That gives you a gentle expression, you see. Do you think — would it be possible — would you advise me to — to — in fact, to shave the hair off my face ?"

The excellent bear looked wistfully at Toto, to mark the effect of this proposition; but Toto, after struggling for some moments to preserve his gravity, burst into a peal of laughter, so loud and clear that it woke the echoes of the forest.

"Ha! ha! ha!" laughed the boy. "Ho! oh, dear me! ho! ho! ha! Bruin, dear, you really *must* excuse me, but I cannot help it. Ho! ho! ho!"

Bruin looked hurt and vexed for a moment, but it was only a moment. Toto's laughter was too contagious to be resisted; the worthy bear's features relaxed, and the next instant he was laughing himself, — or coming as near to it as a black bear can.

"I am a foolish old fellow, I suppose!" he said. "We will say no more about it, Toto. But, hark? who is that speaking. It sounded like a crow, only it was too feeble."

They listened, and presently the sound was heard again; and this time it certainly was a faint but distinct "Caw!" and apparently at no great distance from them. The two companions looked about, and soon saw the owner of the voice perched on a stump, and croaking dismally. A more miserable-looking bird was never seen. His feathers drooped in limp disorder, and evidently had not been trimmed for days; his eyes were half-shut, and save when he opened his beak to utter a despairing "Caw!" he might have been mistaken for a stuffed bird,—and a badly stuffed bird at that.

"Hello, friend!" shouted Toto, in his cheery voice. "What is the matter that you look so down in the beak?"

The crow raised his head, and looked sadly at the two strangers. "I am sick," he said, "and I can't get anything to eat for myself or my master."

"Who is your master?" asked the boy.

"He is a hermit," replied the crow. "He lives in a cave near by; but last week he broke his leg, and has not been able to move since then. He has nothing to eat, for he will not touch raw snails, and I cannot find anything else for him. I fear he will die soon, and I shall probably die too."

"Come! come!" said the bear, "don't let me hear any nonsense of that kind. Die, indeed! Here, take that, sir, and don't talk foolishness!"

"That" was neither more nor less than the wing of a roast chicken which Bruin had pulled hastily from the basket. The famished crow fell upon it, beak and claw, without more ado; and a silence ensued, while the two friends, well pleased, watched the first effect of their charitable mission.

"Poor creature!" said Toto. "Were you ever so hungry as that, Bruin?"

"Oh, yes!" said the bear, carelessly, "often and often. When I came out in the spring, you know. But I never stayed hungry very long," he added, with a significant grimace. "This crow is sick, you see, and probably cannot help himself much. How does that go, old fellow?" he said, addressing the crow, who had polished the chicken-bone till it shone again, and now looked up with a twinkle in his eyes very different from the wretched, lacklustre expression they had at first worn.

"You have given me life, sir!" he said warmly; "you have positively given me life. I am once more a crow' And now, tell me how I can serve you, for you are evidently bent on some errand."

"We have come to see your master," said Toto. "We heard of his accident, and thought he must be in need of help. So, if you will show us the way—"

The crow needed no more, but joyfully spread his wings, and half hopped, half fluttered along the ground as fast as he could go. "Noble strangers!" he cried, "our humble dwelling is close at hand. Follow me, I pray you, and blessings attend your footsteps."

The two friends followed, and soon came upon the entrance to a cave, around which a sort of rustic porch had been built. Vines were trained over it, and a rude chair and table stood beneath the pleasant shade.

"This is my master's study," said the crow. "Here we have spent many happy and profitable hours. May it please you to enter, worshipful sirs?"

"What do you say, Bruin?" asked Toto, glancing at his companion. "Shall we go in, or send the crow first, to announce us?"

"You had better go in alone," said the bear, decidedly. "I will stay here with Master Crow, and when — that is, *if* you think it best for me to come in, later, you have but to call me."

Accordingly Toto entered the cavern, which was dimly lighted by a hole in the roof. As soon as his eyes became accustomed to the gloom, he perceived a rude pallet at one side, on which was stretched the form of a tall old man. His long white hair and beard were matted and tangled; his thin hands lay helpless by his side ; it seemed as if he were scarcely alive. He opened his eyes, however, at the sound of footsteps, and looked half-fearfully at the boy, who bent softly over him.

"Good morning, sir!" said Toto, not knowing what else to say. "Is your leg better, to-day ?"

"Water !" murmured the old man, feebly.

"Water? Why, yes, of course! I 'll get some in a minute."

He started for the mouth of the cave, but before he reached it, a huge, shaggy, black paw was thrust in at the aperture, holding out a bark dish, while a sort of enormous whisper, which just *was* not a growl, murmured, "Here it is !"

"Thank you, Bru — I mean, thank you !" said Toto, in some confusion, glancing apprehensively toward the bed. But the old man noticed nothing, till the clear cool water was held to his lips. He drank eagerly, and seemed to gain a little strength at once, for he now gazed earnestly at Toto, and presently said, in a feeble voice : —

" Who are you, dear child, and what good angel has sent you to save my life ? "

" My name is Toto," replied the boy. " As to how I came here, I will tell you all that by-and-by ; but now you are too weak either to talk or to listen, and I must see at once about getting you some — "

" *Food !* " came the huge whisper again, rolling like a distant muttering of thunder through the cavern; and again the shaggy paw appeared, solemnly waving a bowl of jelly.

Toto flew to take it, but paused for a moment, overcome with amusement at the aspect presented by his friend. The good bear had wedged his huge bulk tightly into a corner behind a jutting fragment of rock. Here he sat, with the basket of provisions between his knees, and an air of deep and solemn mystery in his look and bearing. Not seeing Toto, he still held the bowl of jelly in his outstretched paw, and opening his cavernous jaws, was about to send out another rolling thunder-whisper of "Food !" when Toto sprang quickly on the jelly, and taking a spoon from the basket, rapped the bear on the nose with it, and then returned to his charge.

The poor hermit submitted meekly to being fed with a spoon, and at every mouthful seemed to gain strength. A faint color stole into his wan cheek, his eyes brightened, and before the bowl was two thirds empty, he actually smiled.

"I little thought I should ever taste jelly again," he said. "Indeed, I had fully made up my mind that I must starve to death here; for I was unable to move, and never thought of human aid coming to me in this lonely spot. Even my poor crow, my faithful companion for many years, has left me. I trust he has found some other shelter, for he was feeble and lame, himself."

"Oh, he is all right!" said Toto, cheerily. "It was he who showed us the way here; and he's outside now, talking to — that is — talking to himself, you know."

"Showed *us* the way?" repeated the hermit. "You have a companion, then? Why does he not come in, and let me thank him also for his kindness?"

"He?" said Toto, stammering. "He — oh — he — he does n't like to be thanked."

"But at least he will come in!" urged the old man. "Do, pray, ask him! I am distressed to think of his staying outside. Is he a very shy boy?"

"He is n't a boy," said Toto. "He's — oh! what a muddle I'm making of it! He's bigger than a boy, sir, a great deal bigger. And — I hope you wont mind, but — he's black!"

"A negro! is it possible?" exclaimed the hermit. "My dear boy, I have no prejudice against the Ethiopian race. I must insist on his coming in. Stay! I will call him myself. I believe they are generally called either Cæsar or Pompey. Mr. Pomp — "

"Oh, stop!" cried Toto, in distress. "His name *is n't* Pompey, it's Bruin. And he would n't come in yet if I were to — "

"Cut him into inch pieces!" came rolling like muffled thunder through the doorway.

The old hermit started as if he had been shot. "Ah! what is that?" he cried. "Boy! boy! who — *what* is that speaking?"

"Oh, dear!" cried Toto, distractedly. "Oh, dear! what shall I do? Please don't be alarmed, Mr. Baldhead — I mean, Mr. Hermit. He is the best, dearest, kindest old fellow *in the world*, and it is n't his fault, because he was —"

"Born so!" resounded from without; and the poor hermit, now speechless with terror, could only gasp, and gaze at Toto with eyes of agonized entreaty.

"Yes, he was born so!" continued the boy. "And we might have been bears ourselves, you know, if we had happened to have them for fathers and mothers; so —" But here he paused in dismay, for the hermit, without more ado, quietly fainted away.

"Oh, Bruin! Crow! come here!" cried Toto. "I am afraid he is dead, or dying. What shall we do?"

At this summons the crow came hopping and fluttering in, followed by the unhappy bear, who skulked along, hugging the wall and making himself as small as possible, while he cast shamefaced and apologetic glances toward the bed.

"Oh, you need n't mind now!" cried Toto. "He won't know you are here. Do you think he is dead, Crow? Have you ever seen him like this before?"

But the crow never had; and the three were standing beside the bed in mute dismay, when suddenly a light flutter of wings was heard, and a soft voice cooed, "Toto! Bruin!" and the next moment Pigeon Pretty came flying into the cave, with a bunch of dried leaves in her bill. A glance showed her the situation, and alighting softly on the old man's breast she held the leaves to his nostrils, fanning him the while with her outspread wings.

"Oh!" she said, "I have flown so fast I am quite out of breath. You see, dears, I was afraid that something of this sort might happen, as soon as I heard of your going. I was in the barn, you know, when you were talking about it, and getting ready. So I flew to my old nest and got these leaves, of which I always keep a store on hand. See, he is beginning to revive already."

In truth, the pungent fragrance of the leaves, which now filled the air, seemed to have a magical effect on the sick man. His eyelids fluttered, his lips moved, and he muttered faintly, "The bear! oh, the bear!"

The wood-pigeon motioned to Bruin and Toto to withdraw, which they speedily did, casting remorseful glances at one another. Silently and sadly they sat down in the porch, and here poor Bruin abandoned himself to despair, clutching his shaggy hair, and even pulling out several handfuls of it, while he inwardly called himself by every hard name he could think of. Toto sat looking gloomily at his boots for a long time, but finally he said, in a whisper: —

"Cheer up, old fellow! it was all my fault. I do suppose I am the stupidest boy that ever lived. If I had only managed a little better — hark! what is that?"

Both listened, and heard the soft voice of the wood-pigeon calling, "Bruin! Bruin! Toto! come in, both of you. Mr. Hermit understands all about it now, and is ready to welcome *both* his visitors."

Much amazed, the two friends rose, and slowly and hesitatingly re-entered the cave, the bear making more desperate efforts even than before to conceal his colossal bulk. To his astonishment, however, the hermit, who was now lying propped up by an improvised pillow of dry moss, greeted him with an unflinching gaze, and even smiled and held out his hand.

"Mr. Bruin," he said, "I am glad to meet you, sir! This sweet bird has told me all about you, and I am sincerely pleased to make your acquaintance. So you have walked ten miles and more to bring help and comfort to an old man who stole your honey!"

But this was more than the good bear could stand. He sat down on the ground, and thrusting his great shaggy paws into his eyes, fairly began to blubber. At this, I am ashamed to say, all the others fell to laughing. First, Toto laughed — but Toto,

bless him! was always laughing; and then
Pigeon Pretty laughed; and then Jim Crow;
and then the hermit; and finally, Bruin himself. And so they all laughed together, till
the forest echoes rang, and the woodchucks
almost stirred in their holes.

CHAPTER IX.

IT was late in the afternoon of the same
day. In the cottage at home all was
quiet and peaceful. The grandmother was
taking a nap in her room, with the squirrel
curled up comfortably on the pillow beside
her. In the kitchen, the fire and the kettle
were having it all their own way, for though
two other members of the family were in the
room, they were either asleep or absorbed in
their own thoughts, for they gave no sign of
their presence. The kettle was in its glory,
for Bruin had polished it that very morning, and it shone like the good red gold.
It sang its merriest song, and puffed out
clouds of snow-white steam from its slender
spout.

"Look at me!" it said to the fire. "Am I
not well worth looking at? I feel almost

sure that I must have turned into gold, for I never used to look like this. A golden kettle is rather a rare thing, I flatter myself. It really seems a pity that there is no one here except the stupid parrot, who has gone to sleep, and that odious raccoon, who always looks at me as if I were a black pot, and a cracked pot at that."

"To be sure!" crackled the fire, encouragingly. "To be sure! But never mind, my dear! I admire you immensely, as you know, and it is my greatest pleasure to see myself reflected in your bright face. Crick! crack! cr-r-r-r-rickety!" said the fire.

"Hm! hm! tsing! tsing! tsing!" sang the kettle. And they performed really a very creditable duet together.

Now it happened that the parrot was not asleep, though she had had the bad taste to turn her back on the fire and the kettle. She was looking out of the window, in fact, and wondering when the wood-pigeon would come back. Though not a bird of specially affectionate nature, Miss Mary was still very fond of Pigeon Pretty, and always missed her when she was away. This afternoon had seemed particularly long, for no one had been in the kitchen save Coon, with whom she was not on very good terms. Now, she thought, it was surely time for her friend to return; and she stretched her neck, and peered out of the window, hoping to catch the flutter of the soft brown wings. Instead of this, however, she caught sight of something else, which made her start and ruffle up her feathers, and look again with a very different expression.

Outside the cottage stood a man, — an ill-looking fellow, with a heavy pack strapped on his back. He was looking all about him, examining the outside of the cottage carefully, and evidently listening for any sound that might come from within. All being silent, he stepped to the window (not Miss Mary's window, but the other), and took a long survey of the kitchen; and then, seeing no living creature in it (for the raccoon under the table and the parrot on her perch were both hidden from his view), he laid down his pack, opened the door, and quietly stepped in. An ill-looking fellow, Miss Mary had thought him at the first glance; but now, as she noiselessly turned on her perch and looked more closely at him, she thought his aspect positively villanous. He had a hooked nose and a straggling red beard, and his little green eyes twinkled with an evil light as he looked about the cosey kitchen, with all its neat and comfortable appointments.

First he stepped to the cupboard, and after examining its contents he drew out a mutton-bone (which had been put away for Bruin), a hunch of bread, and a cranberry tart, on which he proceeded to make a hearty meal, without troubling himself about knife· or fork. He ate hurriedly, looking about him the while, — though, curiously enough, he saw neither of the two pairs of bright eyes which were following his every movement. The parrot on her perch sat motionless, not a feather stirring; the raccoon under the table lay crouched against the wall, as still as if he were carved in stone. Even the kettle had stopped singing, and only sent out a low, perturbed murmur from time to time.

His meal finished, the rascal — his confidence increasing as the moments went by without interruption — proceeded to warm himself well by the fire, and then on tiptoe to walk about the room, peering into cupboards and lockers, opening boxes and pulling out drawers. The parrot's blood boiled with indignation at the sight of this "unfeathered vulture," as she mentally termed him, ransacking all the Madam's tidy and well-kept stores; but when he opened the drawer in which lay the six silver teaspoons (the pride of the cottage), and the porringer that Toto had inherited from his great-grandfather, — when he opened this drawer, and with a low whistle of satisfaction drew the precious treasures from their resting-place, Miss Mary could contain herself no longer, but clapped her wings and cried in a clear distinct voice, "Stop thief!"

The man started violently, and dropping the silver back into the drawer, looked about him in great alarm. At first he saw no one, but presently his eyes fell on the parrot, who sat boldly facing him, her yellow eyes gleaming with anger. His terror changed to fury, and with a muttered oath he stepped forward.

"It was you, was it?" he said fiercely. "You'll never say 'Stop thief' again, my fine bird, for I'll wring your neck before I'm half a minute older."

He stretched his hand toward the parrot, who for her part prepared to fly at him and fight for her life; but at that moment something happened. There was a rushing in the air; there was a yell as if a dozen wild-cats had broken loose, and a heavy body fell on the robber's back, — a body which had teeth and claws (an endless number of claws, it seemed, and all as sharp as daggers); a body which yelled and scratched and bit and tore, till the ruffian, half mad with terror and pain, yelled louder than his assailant. Vainly

But at this last mishap the robber, now fairly beside himself, rushed headlong
from the cottage. — PAGE 163.

trying to loosen the clutch of those iron claws, the wretch staggered backward against the hob. Was it accident, or did the kettle by design give a plunge, and come down with a crash, sending a stream of boiling water over his legs? Who can tell? It was a remarkable kettle. But at this last mishap the robber, now fairly beside himself, rushed headlong from the cottage, and still bearing his terrible burden, fled screaming down the road.

At the same moment the door of the grandmother's room was opened hurriedly, and the old lady cried, in a trembling voice, " What has happened? What is it? Coon! Mary! are you here?"

" I am here, Madam!" replied the parrot, quickly. " Coon has — has just stepped out, with — in fact, with an acquaintance. He will be back directly, no doubt."

"But that fearful noise !" said the grandmother. Was that—"

" The acquaintance, dear Madam!" replied Miss Mary, calmly. "He was excited!

—about something, and he raised his voice, I confess, higher than good breeding usually allows. Yes. Have you had a pleasant nap?"

The good old lady, still much mystified, though her fears were set at rest by the parrot's quiet confidence, returned to her room to put on her cap, and to smooth the pretty white curls which her Toto loved. No sooner was the door closed than the squirrel, who had been fairly dancing up and down with curiosity and eagerness, opened a fire of questions: —

"Who was it? What happened? What did he want? Who knocked down the kettle? Why did n't you want Madam to know?" etc.

Miss Mary entered into a full account of the thrilling adventure, and had but just finished it when in walked the raccoon, his eyes sparkling, his tail cocked in its airiest way.

"Well?" cried the parrot, eagerly, "is he gone?"

"Yes, my dear, he is gone!" replied Coon,

gayly. "Oh, dear me! what a pleasant ride I have had! Why did n't you come too, Miss Mary? You might have held on by his hair. It would have been such fun! Yes, I went on quite a good bit with him, just to show him the way, you know. And then I bade him good-by, and begged him to come again; but he did n't say he would."

Coon shook himself, and fairly chuckled with glee, as did also his two companions; but presently Miss Mary, quitting her perch, flew to the table, and holding out her claw to the raccoon, said gravely : —

"Coon, you have saved my life, and perhaps the Madam's and Cracker's too. Give me your paw, and receive my warmest thanks for your timely aid. We have not been the best of friends, lately," she added, "but I trust all will be different now. And the next time you are invited to a party, if you fancy a feather or so to complete your toilet, you have only to mention it, and I shall be happy to oblige you."

"And for my part, Miss Mary," responded

the raccoon warmly, "I beg you to consider me the humblest of your servants from this day forth. If you fancy any little relish, such as snails or fat spiders, as a change from your every-day diet, it will be a pleasure to me to procure them for you. Beauty," he continued, with his most gallant bow, "is enchanting, and valor is enrapturing; but beauty and valor *combined*, are — "

"Oh, come!" said the squirrel, who felt rather crusty, perhaps, because he had not seen the fun, and so did not care for the fine speeches, "stop bowing and scraping to each other, you two, and let us put this distracted-looking room in order before Madam comes in again. Pick up the kettle, will you, Coon? Look! the water is running all over the floor."

The raccoon did not answer, being apparently very busy setting the chairs straight; so Cracker repeated his request, in a sharper voice.

"Do you hear me, Coon? Please pick up that kettle. I cannot do it myself, for it is twice as big as I am, but I should think you could lift it easily, now that it is empty."

The raccoon threw a perturbed glance at the kettle, and then said in a tone which tried to be nonchalant, "Oh! the kettle is all right. It will get up, I suppose, when it feels like it. If it should ask me to help it, of course I would; but perhaps it may prefer the floor for a change. I — I often lie on the floor, myself," he added.

The squirrel stared. "What do you mean?" he said. "It isn't alive! Toto said it wasn't."

The raccoon beckoned him aside, and said in a low tone, "My good Cracker, Toto *says* a great many things, and no doubt he thinks they are all true. But he is a young boy, and, let me tell you, he does *not* know everything in the world. If that thing is not alive, why did it jump off its seat just at the critical moment, and pour hot water over the robber's legs?"

"Did it?" exclaimed the squirrel, much impressed.

"Yes, it did!" replied the raccoon, emphatically. "I saw it with these eyes. And I don't deny that it was a great help, Cracker, and that I was very glad the kettle did it. But see, now! when a creature has no more self-respect than to lie there for a quarter of an hour, with its head on the other side of the room, without making the smallest attempt to get up and put itself together again, why, I tell you frankly *I* don't feel much like assisting it. You never knew one of *us* to behave in that sort of way, did you, now?"

"N-n-no!" said Cracker, doubtfully. "But then, if any of us were to lose our heads, we should be dead, should n't we?"

"Exactly!" cried the raccoon, triumphantly. "And when that thing loses its head, it *is n't* dead. That's just the difference. It can go without it's head for an hour! I've seen it, when Toto took it off — the head, I mean — and forgot to put it on again. I tell you, it just *pretends* to be dead, so that it can be taken care of, and carried about like a baby, and given water whenever it is thirsty.

A secret, underhand, sly creature, I call it, and I sha'n't touch it to put its head on again!"

And that was all the thanks the kettle got for its pains.

CHAPTER X.

WHEN Toto came home, as he did just when night was closing in around the little cottage, he was whistling merrily, as usual; and the first sound of his clear and tuneful whistle brought Coon, Cracker, and Miss Mary all running to the door, to greet, to tell, and to warn him. The boy listened wide-eyed to the story of the attempted robbery, and at the end of it he drew a long breath of relief.

"I am *so* glad you didn't let Granny know!" he cried. "That was clever of you. She never would have slept quietly again. And, I say! what a good fellow you are, Coon! Shake paws, old boy! And Miss Mary, you are a trump, and I would give you a golden nose-ring like your Princess's if you had a nose to wear it on. To think of you two defending the castle, and putting the enemy to. flight, horse, foot, and dragoons ! "

" What is dragoons ? " asked the parrot, gravely. " I don't think he had any about him, unless it was concealed. He had no horse, either; but he had two feet, — and very ugly ones they were. He danced on them when the kettle poured hot water over his legs, — danced higher than ever you did, Toto."

" Did he ? " laughed Toto, who was in high spirits. " Ha ! ha ! I am delighted to hear it. But," he added, " it is so dark that you do not see our guest, whom I have brought home for a little visit. Where are you, Jim Crow ? Come here and be introduced to the family ! "

Thus adjured, the crow hopped solemnly forward, and made his best bow to the three inmates, who in turn saluted him, each after his or her fashion. The raccoon was gracious and condescending, the squirrel familiar and friendly, the parrot frigidly polite, though inwardly resenting that a crow should be presented to her, — to *her*, the favorite attendant of the late lamented Princess of Central Africa, — without her permission having been asked first. As for the crow, he stood on one leg and blinked at them all in a manner which meant a great deal or nothing at all, just as you chose to take it.

"Distinguished persons!" he said, gravely, "it is with pleasure that I make your acquaintance. May this day be the least happy of your lives! Lady Parrot," he added, addressing himself particularly to Miss Mary, "grant me the honor of leading you within. The evening air is chill for one so delicate and fragile."

Miss Mary, highly delighted at being addressed by such a stately title as "Lady Parrot," relaxed at once the severity of her mien, and gracefully sidled into the house in company with the sable-clad stranger, while Toto and the two others followed, much amused.

After a hearty supper, in the course of which Toto related as much of his and Bruin's adventures in the hermit's cave as he thought proper, the whole family gathered around the blazing hearth. Toto brought the pan of apples and the dish of nuts; the grandmother took up her knitting, and said, with a smile: "And who will tell us a story, this evening? We have had none for two evenings now, and it is high time that we heard something new. Cracker, my dear, is it not your turn?"

"I think it is," said the squirrel, hastily cramming a couple of very large nuts into his cheek-pouches, "and if you like, I will tell you a story that Mrs. Cow told me a day or two ago. It is about a cow that jumped over the moon."

"What!" cried Toto. "Why, I 've known that story ever since I was a baby! And it is n't a story, either, it's a rhyme, —

> "Hey diddle diddle,
> The cat and the fiddle,
> The cow — "

"Yes, yes! I know, Toto," interrupted the squirrel. "She told me that, too, and said it was a pack of lies, and that people like you

did n't know anything about the real truth of
the matter.   So now, if you will just listen to
me, I will tell you how it really happened."

THE MOON-CALF.

There once was a young cow, and she had
a calf.

"And that's half!" said Toto, in rather a
provoking manner.

"No, it is n't, it's only the beginning,"
said the little squirrel, indignantly; "and if
you would rather tell the story yourself, Toto,
you are welcome to do so."

"Beg pardon! Crackey," said Toto, apologetically. "Won't do so again, Crackey;
go on, that's a dear!" and the squirrel, who
never bore malice for more than two minutes,
put his little huff away, and continued : —

This young cow, you see, she was very fond
of her calf, — very fond indeed she was, —
and when they took it away from her, she
was very unhappy, and went about roaring
all day long.

"Cows don't roar!" said Toto the irrepressible. "They *low*. There's a piece of poetry about it that I learned once: —

"'The lowing herd —'

do something or other, I don't remember what."

"'The lowing herd winds slowly o'er the lea,'

quoted the grandmother, softly.

"What do they wind?" asked the raccoon. "Yarn, or a chain-pump like the one in the yard, or what?"

"I don't know what you mean by *low*, Toto!" said the squirrel, without noticing Coon's remarks. "Your cow roared so loud the other day that I fell off her horn into the hay. I don't see anything *low* in that."

"Why, Cracker, can't you understand?" cried Toto. "They *low* when they *moo!* I don't mean that they moo *low*, but 'moo' *is* 'low,' don't you see?"

"No, I do *not* see!" replied the squirrel, stoutly. "And I don't believe there is anything *to* see, I don't. So there, now!"

At this point Madam interfered, and with a few gentle words made the matter clear, and smoothed the ruffled feathers — or rather fur.

The raccoon, who had been listening with ears pricked up, and keen eyes glancing from one to the other of the disputants, now murmured, "Ah, yes! very explicit. Quite what I should have said myself!" and relapsed into his former attitude of graceful and dignified ease.

The squirrel repeated to himself, "Moo! low! loo! mow! moo!" several times, shook his head, refreshed himself with a nut, and finally, at the general request, continued his story :

So, as I said, this young cow was very sad, and she looed — I mean mowed — all day to express her grief. And she thought, "If I could only know where my calf is, it would not be quite so dreadfully bad. But they would not tell me where they were taking him, though I asked them politely in seven different tones, which is more than any other cow here can use."

Now, when she was thinking these thoughts it chanced that the maid came to milk the cows, and with the maid came a young man, who was talking very earnestly to her.

"What is it, Molly?" says he. "Does n't thee know me well enough?"

"I knows a moon-calf when I sees him!" says the maid; and with that she boxed his ears, and sat down to milk the cow, and he went away in a huff.

But the cow heard what the maid said, and began to wonder what moon-calves were, and whether they were anything like her calf. Presently, when the maid had gone away with the pail of milk, she said to the Oldest Ox, who happened to be standing near, —

"Old Ox, pray tell me, what is a moon-calf?"

The Oldest Ox did not know anything about moon-calves, but he had no idea of betraying his ignorance to anybody, much less to a very young cow; so he answered promptly, "It 's a calf that lives in the moon, of course."

"Is it — are they — like other calves?" inquired the cow, timidly, "or a different sort of animal?"

"When a creature is called a calf," replied the Ox, severely, "it *is* a calf. If it were a cat, a hyena, or a toad with three tails, it would be called by its own name. Now do you understand?"

Then he shut his eyes and pretended to be asleep, for he did not like to answer questions on matters of which he knew nothing; it fatigued his brain, and oxen should always avoid fatigue of the brain.

But the young cow had one more question to ask, and could not rest till it was answered; so mustering all her courage, she said, desperately, "Oh, Old Ox! before you go to sleep, please — *please*, tell me if people ever take calves to the moon from here?"

"Frequently!" said the Oldest Ox. "I wish you were there, now. I am asleep. Good-night to you!" and in a few minutes he really was asleep.

But the young cow stood still, thinking.

She thought so hard that when the farmer's boy came to drive the cattle into the barn, she hardly saw where she was going, but stumbled first against the door and then against the wall, and finally walked into Old Brindle's stall instead of her own, and got well prodded by the latter's horns in consequence.

"This cow is sick!" said the farmer's boy. "I must give her a warm mash, and cut an inch or two off her tail to-morrow."

Next day the cows were driven out into the pasture, for the weather was warm, and they found it a pleasant change from the barn-yard. They cropped the honey-clover, well seasoned with buttercups and with just enough dandelions scattered about to "give it character," as Mother Brindle said. They stood knee-deep in the cool, clear stream which flowed under the willows, and lay down in the shade of the great oak-tree, and altogether were as happy as cows can possibly be.

All but the young red cow. She cared nothing for any of the pleasures which she had once enjoyed so keenly; she only walked up and down, up and down, thinking of her lost calf, and looking for the moon. For she had fully made up her mind by this time that her darling Bossy had been taken to the moon, and had become a moon-calf; and she was wondering whether she might not see or hear something of him when the moon rose.

The day passed, and when the evening was still all rosy in the west, a great globe of shining silver rose up in the east. It was the full moon, coming to take the place of the sun, who had put on his nightcap and gone to bed. The young cow ran towards it, stretching out her neck, and calling, —

"Bossy! Moo! moo! Bossy, are you there?"

Then she listened, and thought she heard a distant voice which said, "There!"

"I knew it!" she cried, frantically, "I knew it! Bossy is now a moon-calf. Something must be done about it at once, if I only knew what!"

And she ran to Mother Brindle, who was standing by the fence, talking to the neighbor's black cow, — her with the spotted nose.

"Mother Brindle!" she cried. "Have you ever had a calf taken to the moon? My calf, my Bossy, is there, and is now a moon-calf. Tell me, oh! tell me, how to get at him, I beseech you!"

"What nonsense is this?" said Mother Brindle, severely. "Compose yourself! You are excited, and will injure your milk, and that would reflect upon the whole herd. As for your calf, why should you be better off than other people? I have lost ten calves, the finest that ever were seen, and I never made half such a fuss about them as you make over this puny little red creature."

"But he is *there*, in the moon!" cried the poor cow. "I must find him and get him down. I *must*, do you hear?"

"Decidedly, your wits must be in the moon, my dear," said the neighbor's black cow, not unkindly. "They certainly have left you. Who ever heard of calves in the moon? Not I, for one; and I am not more ignorant than others, perhaps."

The red cow was about to reply, when

suddenly across the meadow came ringing the farm-boy's call, "Co, Boss! Co, Boss! Co, Boss!"

"Ah!" said Mother Brindle, "can it really be milking-time? What a pleasant day this has been! Good-evening to you, neighbor. And you, child," she added, turning to the red cow, "come straight home with me. I heard James promise you a warm mash, and that will be the best thing for you."

But at these words the young cow started, and with a wild bellow ran to the farthest end of the pasture. "Bossy!" she cried, staring wildly up at the silver globe, which was rising steadily higher and higher in the sky, "you are going away from me! Jump down from the moon, and come to your mother! Bossy! Bossy! *Come!*"

And then a distant voice, floating softly down through the air, answered, "Come! come!"

"He calls me!" cried the red cow. "My darling calls me, and I go. I will go to the moon; I will be a moon-cow! Bossy, Bossy, I come!"

She ran forward like an antelope, gave a sudden leap into the air, and went up, up, up, — over the haystacks, over the trees, over the clouds, — up among the stars.

But, alas! in her frantic desire to reach the moon she overshot the mark; jumped clear over it, and went down on the other side, nobody knows where, and she never was seen or heard of again.

And Mother Brindle, when she saw what had happened, ran straight home and gobbled up the warm mash before any of the other cows could get there, and ate so fast that she made herself ill.

"That is the whole story," said the squirrel, seriously; "and it seemed to me a very curious one, I confess."

"Very!" said Toto, dryly. "But there's nothing about the others in it, — the cat and fiddle, and the little dog, you know."

"Well, they *were n't* in it really, at all!" replied Cracker. "They were all lies, Mrs. Cow says, every one of them."

"Humph!" said Toto "Well, Mrs. Cow ought to be a good judge of lies, I should say."

"What can be expected," said the raccoon loftily, "from a creature who eats hay? Be good enough to hand me those nuts, Toto, will you? The story has positively made me hungry, — a thing that has not happened — "

"Since dinner-time!" said Toto. "Wonderful indeed, Coon! But I shall hand the nuts to Cracker first, for he has told us a very good story, whether it is true or not."

CHAPTER XI.

THE apples and nuts went round again and again, and for a few minutes nothing was heard save the cracking of shells and the gnawing of sharp white teeth. At length the parrot said, meditatively : —

"That was a very stupid cow, though! Are all cows as stupid as that?"

"Well, I don't think they are what you would call brilliant, as a rule," Toto admitted; "but they are generally good, and that is better."

"Hem! possibly!" said Miss Mary, dryly. "That is probably why we have no cows in Central Africa. Our animals being all, without exception, clever *and* good, there is really no place for creatures of the sort you describe."

"How about the bogghun, Miss Mary?"

asked the raccoon, slyly, with a wink at Toto.

The parrot ruffled up her feathers, and was about to make a sharp reply; but suddenly remembering the raccoon's brave defence of her an hour before, she smoothed her plumage again, and replied gently, —

"I confess that I forgot the bogghun, Coon. It is indeed a treacherous and a wicked creature! — a dark blot on the golden roll of African animals." She paused and sighed, then added, as if to change the subject, "But, come! is it too late to have another story? If not, I have a short one in mind, which I will tell you, if you wish."

All assented joyfully, and Miss Mary, without more delay, related the story of

THE THREE REMARKS.

There was once a princess, the most beautiful princess that ever was seen. Her hair was black and soft as the raven's wing [here the Crow blinked, stood on one leg and plumed himself, evidently highly flattered by the allusion]; her eyes were like stars dropped in a pool of clear water, and her speech like the first tinkling cascade of the baby Nile. She was also wise, graceful, and gentle, so that one would have thought she must be the happiest princess in the world.

But, alas! there was one terrible drawback to her happiness. She could make only three remarks. No one knew whether it was the fault of her nurse, or a peculiarity born with her; but the sad fact remained, that no matter what was said to her, she could only reply in one of three phrases. The first was, —

"What is the price of butter?"

The second, "Has your grandmother sold her mangle yet?"

And the third, "With all my heart!"

You may well imagine what a great misfortune this was to a young and lively princess. How could she join in the sports and dances of the noble youths and maidens of the court? She could not always be silent, neither could she always say, "With all my heart!" though this was her favorite phrase, and she used it whenever she possibly could; and it was not at all pleasant, when some gallant knight asked her whether she would rather play croquet or Aunt Sally, to be obliged to reply, "What is the price of butter?"

On certain occasions, however, the princess actually found her infirmity of service to her. She could always put an end suddenly to any conversation that did not please her, by interposing with her first or second remark; and they were also a very great assistance to her when, as happened nearly every day, she received an offer of marriage. Emperors, kings, princes, dukes, earls, marquises, viscounts, baronets, and many other lofty personages knelt at her feet, and offered her their hands, hearts, and other possessions of greater or less value. But for all her suitors the princess had but one answer. Fixing her deep radiant eyes on them, she would reply with thrilling earnestness, "*Has* your grandmother sold her mangle yet?" and this always impressed the suitors so deeply that they retired weeping to a neighboring monastery, where they hung up their armor in the chapel, and taking the vows, passed the remainder of their lives mostly in flogging themselves, wearing hair shirts, and putting dry toast-crumbs in their beds.

Now, when the king found that all his best nobles were turning into monks, he was greatly displeased, and said to the princess: —

"My daughter, it is high time that all this nonsense came to an end. The next time a respectable person asks you to marry him, you will say, 'With all my heart!' or I will know the reason why."

But this the princess could not endure, for she had never yet seen a man whom she was willing to marry. Nevertheless, she feared her father's anger, for she knew that he always kept his word; so that very night she slipped down the back stairs of the palace, opened the back door, and ran away out into the wide world.

She wandered for many days, over mountain and moor, through fen and through forest, until she came to a fair city. Here all the bells were ringing, and the people shouting and flinging caps into the air; for their old king was dead, and they were just about to crown a new one. The new king was a stranger, who had come to the town only the day before; but as soon as he heard of the old monarch's death, he told the people that he was a king himself, and as he happened to be without a kingdom at that moment, he would be quite willing to rule over them. The people joyfully assented, for the late king had left no heir; and now all the preparations had been completed. The crown had been polished up, and a new tip put on the sceptre, as the old king had quite spoiled it by poking the fire with it for upwards of forty years.

When the people saw the beautiful princess, they welcomed her with many bows, and insisted on leading her before the new king.

"Who knows but that they may be related?" said everybody. "They both came from the same direction, and both are strangers."

Accordingly the princess was led to the market-place, where the king was sitting in royal state. He had a fat, red, shining face, and did not look like the kings whom she had been in the habit of seeing; but nevertheless the princess made a graceful courtesy, and then waited to hear what he would say.

The new king seemed rather embarrassed when he saw that it was a princess who appeared before him; but he smiled graciously, and said, in a smooth oily voice, —

"I trust your 'Ighness is quite well. And 'ow did yer 'Ighness leave yer pa and ma?"

At these words the princess raised her head and looked fixedly at the red-faced king; then she replied, with scornful distinctness, —

"What is the price of butter?"

At these words an alarming change came over the king's face. The red faded from it, and left it a livid green; his teeth chattered; his eyes stared, and rolled in their sockets; while the sceptre dropped from his trembling hand and fell at the princess's feet. For the truth was, this was no king at all, but a retired butterman, who had laid by a little money at his trade, and had thought of setting up a public house; but chancing to pass through this city at the very time when they were looking for a king, it struck him that he might just as well fill the vacant place as any one else. No one had thought of his being an impostor; but when the princess fixed her clear eyes on him and asked him that familiar question, which he had been in the habit of hearing many times a day for a great part of his life, the guilty butterman thought himself detected, and shook in his guilty shoes. Hastily descending from his throne, he beckoned the princess into a side-chamber, and closing the door, besought her in moving terms not to betray him.

"Here," he said, "is a bag of rubies as big as pigeon's eggs. There are six thousand of them, and I 'umbly beg your 'Ighness to haccept them as a slight token hof my hesteem, if your 'Ighness will kindly consent to spare a respeckable tradesman the disgrace of being hexposed."

The princess reflected, and came to the conclusion that, after all, a butterman might make as good a king as any one else; so she took the rubies with a gracious little nod, and departed, while all the people shouted, "Hooray!" and followed her, waving their hats and kerchiefs, to the gates of the city.

With her bag of rubies over her shoulder, the fair princess now pursued her journey, and fared forward over heath and hill, through brake and through brier. After several days she came to a deep forest, which she entered without hesitation, for she knew no fear. She had not gone a hundred paces under the arching limes, when she was met by a band of robbers, who stopped her and asked what she did in their forest, and what she carried in her bag. They were fierce, black-bearded men, armed to the teeth with daggers, cutlasses, pistols, dirks, hangers, blunderbusses, and other defensive weapons; but the princess gazed calmly on them, and said haughtily, —

"Has your grandmother sold her mangle yet?"

The effect was magical. The robbers started back in dismay, crying, "The countersign!" Then they hastily lowered their weapons, and assuming attitudes of abject humility, besought the princess graciously to accompany them to their master's presence. With a lofty gesture she signified assent, and the cringing, trembling bandits led her on through the forest till they reached an open glade, into which the sunbeams glanced right merrily. Here, under a broad oak-tree which stood in the centre of the glade, reclined a man of gigantic stature and commanding mien, with a whole armory of weapons displayed upon his person. Hastening to their chief, the robbers conveyed to him, in agitated whispers, the circumstance of their meeting the princess, and of her unexpected reply to their questions. Hardly seeming to credit their statement, the gigantie chieftain sprang to his feet, and advancing toward the princess with a respectful rever-

"It is true!" he gasped. "We are undone! Noble princess!" and here he and the whole band assumed attitudes of supplication. — PAGE 195.

ence, begged her to repeat the remark which had so disturbed his men. With a royal air, and in clear and ringing tones, the princess repeated, —

"*Has* your grandmother sold her mangle yet?" and gazed steadfastly at the robber chief.

He turned deadly pale, and staggered against a tree, which alone prevented him from falling.

"It is true!" he gasped. "We are undone! The enemy is without doubt close at hand, and all is over. Yet," he added with more firmness, and with an appealing glance at the princess, "yet there may be one chance left for us. If this gracious lady will consent to go forward, instead of returning through the wood, we may yet escape with our lives. Noble princess!" and here he and the whole band assumed attitudes of supplication, "consider, I pray you, whether it would really add to your happiness to betray to the advancing army a few poor foresters, who earn their bread by the sweat of their brow.

Here," he continued, hastily drawing something from a hole in the oak-tree, "is a bag containing ten thousand sapphires, each as large as a pullet's egg. If you will graciously deign to accept them, and to pursue your journey in the direction I shall indicate, the Red Chief of the Rustywhanger will be your slave forever."

The princess, who of course knew that there was no army in the neighborhood, and who moreover did not in the least care which way she went, assented to the Red Chief's proposition, and taking the bag of sapphires, bowed her farewell to the grateful robbers, and followed their leader down a ferny path which led to the farther end of the forest. When they came to the open country, the robber chieftain took his leave of the princess, with profound bows and many protestations of devotion, and returned to his band, who were already preparing to plunge into the impenetrable thickets of the midforest.

The princess, meantime, with her two bags

of gems on her shoulders, fared forward with a light heart, by dale and by down, through moss and through meadow. By-and-by she came to a fair high palace, built all of marble and shining jasper, with smooth lawns about it, and sunny gardens of roses and gillyflowers, from which the air blew so sweet that it was a pleasure to breathe it. The princess stood still for a moment, to taste the sweetness of this air, and to look her fill at so fair a spot; and as she stood there, it chanced that the palace-gates opened, and the young king rode out with his court, to go a-catching of nighthawks.

Now when the king saw a right fair princess standing alone at his palace-gate, her rich garments dusty and travel-stained, and two heavy sacks hung upon her shoulders, he was filled with amazement; and leaping from his steed, like the gallant knight that he was, he besought her to tell him whence she came and whither she was going, and in what way he might be of service to her.

But the princess looked down at her little

dusty shoes, and answered never a word; for she had seen at the first glance how fair and goodly a king this was, and she would not ask him the price of butter, nor whether his grandmother had sold her mangle yet. But she thought in her heart, "Now, I have never, in all my life, seen a man to whom I would so willingly say, 'With all my heart!' if he should ask me to marry him."

The king marvelled much at her silence, and presently repeated his questions, adding, "And what do you carry so carefully in those two sacks, which seem over-heavy for your delicate shoulders?"

Still holding her eyes downcast, the princess took a ruby from one bag, and a sapphire from the other, and in silence handed them to the king, for she willed that he should know she was no beggar, even though her shoes were dusty. Thereat all the nobles were filled with amazement, for no such gems had ever been seen in that country.

But the king looked steadfastly at the princess, and said, "Rubies are fine, and sapphires are fair; but, maiden, if I could but see those eyes of yours, I warrant that the gems would look pale and dull beside them."

At that the princess raised her clear dark eyes, and looked at the king and smiled; and the glance of her eyes pierced straight to his heart, so that he fell on his knees and cried:

"Ah! sweet princess, now do I know that thou art the love for whom I have waited so long, and whom I have sought through so many lands. Give me thy white hand, and tell me, either by word or by sign, that thou wilt be my queen and my bride!"

And the princess, like a right royal maiden as she was, looked him straight in the eyes, and giving him her little white hand, answered bravely, "*With all my heart!*"

CHAPTER XII.

NOW, if we had looked into the hermit's cave a few days after this, we should have seen a very pleasant sight. The good old man was sitting up on his narrow couch, with his lame leg on a stool before him. On another stool sat our worthy friend Bruin, with a backgammon-board on his knees, and the two were deep in the mysteries of Russian backgammon.

"Doublets!" said the hermit, throwing the dice.

"Dear, dear, what luck you do have!" said the bear. "Double sixes again! That takes you out, does n't it?"

"Yes," said the hermit, "this finishes the game and the rubber. But just remember, my friend, how you beat me yesterday. I was ´gammoned over and over again, with never a doublet to save me from ruin."

"To be sure!" said Bruin, with a chuckle. "To be sure! yesterday was one of my good days. And so to-day you have gammoned me back again. I suppose that is why the game is called back-gammon, hey?"

"Possibly!" replied the hermit, smiling.

"And how have you been in the habit of playing?" continued the bear. "You spoke of playing last winter, you know. Whom did you play with, for example?"

"With myself," said the hermit, — "the right hand against the left. I taught my crow the game once, but it did n't work very well. He could not lift the dice-box, and could only throw the dice by running against the box, and upsetting it. This was apt to disarrange the pieces, you see; and as he would not trust me to throw for him, we gave it up."

"I see!" said Bruin, thoughtfully. "And what else did you do in the way of amusement?"

"I read, chiefly," replied the old man. "You see I have a good many books, and they are all good ones, which will bear reading many times."

"Humph!" said the bear. "That is *one* thing about you people that I cannot understand, — the reading of books. Seems so senseless, you know, when you can use your eyes for other things. But, tell me," he added, "have you never thought of trying our way of passing the winter? It is certainly much the best way, when one is alone. Choose a comfortable place, like this, for example, curl yourself up in the warmest corner, and there you are, with nothing to do but to sleep till spring comes again."

"I am afraid I could not do that," said the hermit with a smile. "We are made differently, you see. I cannot sleep more than a few hours at a time, at any season of the year."

"Not if you sucked your paw?" inquired the bear, eagerly. "That makes all the difference, you know. Have you ever *tried* sucking your paw?"

The hermit was forced to admit that he never had.

"Ah! well, you really must try it some day," said Bruin. "There is nothing like it, after all. Nothing like it! I will confess to you," he added in a low tone, and looking cautiously about to make sure that they were alone, "that I have missed it sadly this winter. In most respects this has been the happiest season of my life, and I have enjoyed it more than I can tell you; but still there are times, — when I am tired, you know, or the weather is dull, or Coon is a little trying, as he is sometimes, — times when I feel as if I would give a great deal for a quiet corner where I could suck my paw and sleep for a week or two."

"Could n't you manage it, somehow?" asked the hermit, sympathetically.

"Oh, no! no!" replied the good bear, decidedly. "Coon thinks the Madam would not like it. He is very genteel, you know, — very genteel indeed, Coon is; and he says it would n't be at all ' the thing' for me to suck

my paw anywhere about the place. I never
know just what 'thing' he means when he
says that, but it's a favorite expression of
his; and he certainly knows a great deal
about good manners. Besides," he added,
more cheerfully, " there is always plenty of
work to do, and that is the best thing to keep
one awake. But now, Mr. Baldhead, it is
time for your dinner, sir; and here am I
sitting and talking, when I ought to be
warming your broth!"

With these words the excellent bear arose,
put away the backgammon board, and proceeded to build up the fire, hang the kettle,
and put the broth on to warm, all as deftly
as if he had been a cook all his life. He
stirred and tasted, shook his head, tasted
again, and then said, —

"You have n't the top of a young pine-
tree anywhere about the house, I suppose? It would give this broth such a nice
flavor."

"I am afraid not!" said the hermit, laughing. "I don't generally keep a large stock

of such things on hand. But I fancy the broth will be very good without it, to judge from the last I had."

The bear still looked dissatisfied. "Do you ever put frogs in your broth?" he asked, presently. "Whole ones, you know, rolled in a batter, just like dumplings?"

"*No!*" said the hermit, quickly and decidedly. "I am quite sure I should not like them, thank you, — though it was very kind of you to make the suggestion!" he added, seeing that Bruin looked disappointed.

"You have no idea how nice they are," said the good bear, rather sadly. "But you are so strange, you people! I never could induce Toto or Madam to try them, either. I invented the soup myself, — at least the frog-dumpling part of it, — and made it one day as a little surprise for them. But when I told them what the dumplings were, Toto choked and rolled on the floor, and Madam was quite ill at the very thought, though she had not begun to eat her soup. So Coon and Cracker and I had it all to ourselves, and uncommonly good it was. It's a pity for people to be so prejudiced."

The good hermit was choking a little himself, for some reason or other, but he looked very grave when Bruin turned toward him for assent, and said, "Quite so!" which is a safe remark under most circumstances.

The broth being now ready, the bear proceeded to arrange a tray neatly, and set it before his patient, who took up his wooden spoon and fell to with right good-will. The good bear stood watching him with great satisfaction; and it was really a pity that there was no one there to watch the bear himself, for as he stood there with a clean cloth over his arm, his head on one side, and his honest face beaming with pride and pleasure, he was very well worth looking at.

At this moment a sharp cry of terror was heard outside, then a quick whirr of wings, and the next moment the wood-pigeon darted into the cave, closely pursued by a large hawk. Poor Pigeon Pretty! She was quite exhausted, and with one more piteous cry she fell fainting at Bruin's feet. In another instant the hawk would have pounced upon her, but that instant never came for the winged marauder. Instead, something or somebody pounced on *him*. A thick white covering enveloped him, entangling his claws, binding down his wings, well-nigh stifling him. He felt himself seized in an iron grasp and lifted bodily into the air, while a deep, stern voice exclaimed, —

"Now, sir! have you anything to say for yourself, before I wring your neck?"

Then the covering was drawn back from his head, and he found himself face to face with the great bear, whom he knew perfectly well by sight. But he was a bold fellow, too well used to danger to shrink from it, even in so terrible a form as this; and his fierce yellow eyes met the stern gaze of his captor without shrinking.

"Have you anything to say?" repeated the bear, "before I wring your ugly neck?"

"No!" replied the hawk, sullenly, "wring away."

This answer rather disconcerted our friend Bruin, who, as he sometimes said sadly to himself, had "lost all taste for killing;" so he only shook Master Hawk a little, and said, —

"Do you know of any reason why your neck should *not* be wrung?"

"None in life!" answered the hawk. "Wring away, I tell you! Are you afraid, you great clumsy monster?"

"I'll soon show you whether I am afraid or not!" said the bear, sternly. "Why did you chase my pigeon?"

"'Cause I wanted to eat her!" was the defiant reply. "If *you* had had nothing to eat for a week, you'd have eaten her long before this, I'll be bound!"

"Nothing to eat for a week!" repeated the bear, incredulously. "Why was that?"

"'Cause there wasn't anything, stupid!" said the other.

Here Bruin began to rub his nose with his disengaged paw, and to look helplessly about him, as he always did when disturbed in mind.

"Now — now — now!" he exclaimed, "you hawk, what do you mean by that? Could n't you dig for roots?"

The hawk stared. "Dig for roots?" he repeated, contemptuously. "Look at my beak! Do you think I can dig with that?"

"It *is* rather short," said Bruin; "but — yes! why, of course, *any one* can dig, if he wants to."

"Ask that old thing," said the hawk, nodding toward the hermit, "whether *he* ever dug with his beak; and it's twice as long as mine."

"Of course he has!" replied Bruin, promptly; but then he faltered, for it suddenly occurred to him that he had never seen either Toto or the Madam dig with their noses; and it was with some hesitation that he asked:

"Mr. Baldhead — excuse me! but — a — have you ever tried digging for roots in the ground — with your beak — I mean, nose?"

The hermit looked up gravely, as he sat with Pigeon Pretty on his knee. "No, my friend," he said with great seriousness, "I have never tried it, and doubt if I could do it. I can dig with my hands, though," he added, seeing the good bear look more and more puzzled.

"Ah, yes!" said Bruin. "But you see this bird has no hands, though he has very ugly claws; so that does n't help — Well!" he cried, breaking off short, and once more addressing the hawk. "I don't see anything for it *but* to wring your neck, do you? After all, it will keep you from being hungry again."

But here the soft voice of the wood-pigeon interposed. "No, no! Bruin, dear," cried the gentle bird. "Give him something to eat, and let him go. If he had eaten nothing for a week, I am sure he was not to blame for pursuing the first eatable creature he saw. Remember," she added in a lower tone, which only the bear could hear, "that before this winter, any of us would have done the same."

Bruin scratched his head helplessly; the hawk turned his yellow eyes on Pigeon Pretty with a strange look, but said nothing.

But now the hermit saw that it was time for him to interfere.

"Pigeon Pretty," he said, "you are right, as usual. Bruin, my friend, bring your prisoner here, and let him finish this excellent broth, into which I have crumbled some bread. I will answer for Master Hawk's good behavior, for the present at least," he added, "for I know that he comes of an old and honorable family."

Wonder of wonders! In five minutes the hawk was sitting quietly on the hermit's knee, sipping broth, pursuing the floating bits of bread in the bowl, and submitting to have his soft black plumage stroked, with the best grace in the world. On the good man's other knee sat Pigeon Pretty, now quite recovered from her fright and fatigue, her soft eyes beaming with pleasure; while Bruin squatted opposite them, looking from one to the other, and assuring himself over and over again that Pigeon Pretty was " a most astonishing bird ! 'pon my word, a *most* astonishing bird ! "

His meal ended, the stranger wiped his beak politely on his feathers, plumed himself, and thanked his hosts for their hospitality, with a stately courtesy which contrasted strangely with his former sullen and ferocious bearing. The fierce glare was gone from his eyes, which were, however, still strangely bright; and with his glossy plumage smooth, and his head held proudly erect, he really was a noble-looking bird.

"Long is it, indeed," he said, " since any one has spoken a kind word to Ger-Falcon. It will not be forgotten, I assure you. We are a wild and lawless family, — our beak against every one, and every one's claw against us, — and yet, as you observed, Sir Baldhead, we are an old and honorable race. Alas! for the brave, brave days of old, when my sires were the honored companions of kings and princes! My grandfather seventy times removed was served by an emperor, the ob- sequious monarch carrying him every day on his own wrist to the hunting. He ate from a golden dish, and wore a collar of gems about his neck. Ah, me! what would be the feelings of that noble ancestor if he could see his descendant a hunted outlaw, persecuted by the sons of those very men who once courted and caressed him, and supporting a precarious existence by the ignoble spoils of barn-yards and hen-roosts!"

The hawk paused, overcome by these recollections of past glory, and the good bear said kindly, —

"Dear! dear! very sad, I'm sure. And how did this melancholy change come about, pray?"

"Fashion, my dear sir!" replied the hawk, "ignoble fashion! The race of men degenerated, and occupied themselves with less lofty sports than hawking. My family, left to themselves, knew not what to do. They had been trained to pursue, to overtake, to slay, through long generations; they were unfitted for anything else. But when they began to lead this life on their own account, man, always ungrateful, turned upon them, and persecuted them for the very deeds which had once been the delight and pride of his fickle race. So we fell from our high estate, lower and lower, till the present representative of the Ger-Falcon is the poór creature you behold before you."

The hawk bowed in proud humility, and his hearers all felt, perhaps, much more sorry for him than he deserved. The wood-pigeon was about to ask something more about his famous ancestors, when a shadow darkened the mouth of the cave, and Toto made his appearance, with the crow perched on his shoulder.

"Well, Mr. Baldhead!" he cried in his fresh, cheery voice, "how are you to-day, sir? Better still? I have brought you some — hello! who is this?" And catching sight of the stranger, he stopped short, and looked at the bear for an explanation.

"This is Mr. Ger-Falcon, Toto," said Bruin. "My friend Toto, Mr. Falcon." Toto nodded, and the hawk made him a stately bow; but the two looked distrustfully at each other, and neither seemed inclined to make any advances. Bruin continued, —.

"Mr. Falcon came here in a—well, not in a friendly way at all, I must say. But he is in a very different frame of mind, now, and I trust there will be no further trouble."

"Do you ever change your name, sir?" asked Toto, abruptly, addressing the hawk.

"I do not understand you, sir!" replied the latter, haughtily. "I have no reason to be ashamed of my name."

"Perhaps not!" said the boy. "And yet I am tolerably sure that Mr. Ger-Falcon is no other than Mr. Chicken Hawkon, and that it was he who tried to carry off my Black Spanish chickens yesterday morning."

"You are right, sir!" said the hawk. "You are quite right! I was starving, and the chickens presented themselves to me wholly in the light of food. May I ask for what purpose you keep chickens, sir?"

"Why, we eat them when they grow up," said Toto; "but—"

"Ah, precisely!" murmured the hawk. "You eat them also. I thought so."

"But we don't steal other people's chickens," said the boy, "we eat our own."

"Precisely!" said the hawk, again. "You eat the tame, confiding creatures who feed from your hand, and stretch their necks trustfully to meet their doom. I, on the contrary, when the pangs of hunger force me to snatch a morsel of food to save me from starvation, snatch it from strangers, not from my friends."

Toto was about to make a hasty reply, but the bear, with a motion of his paw, checked him, and said gravely to the hawk, —

"Come, come! Mr. Falcon, I cannot have any dispute of this kind. There is some truth in what you say, and I have no doubt that emperors and other disreputable people have had a large share in forming the bad habits into which you and all your family have fallen. But those habits must be changed, sir, if you intend to remain in this forest. You must not meddle with Toto's chickens; you must not chase quiet and harmless birds. You must, in short, become a respectable and law-abiding bird, instead of a robber and a murderer."

"All very fine!" said the hawk, angrily. "But how am I to live, pray? I can be 're-spectable,' as you call it, in summer; but in weather like this—"

"That can be easily managed," said the kind hermit. "You can stay with me, Falcon. I shall soon be able to shift for myself, and I will gladly undertake to feed you until the snow and frost are gone. You will be a companion for my crow— By the way, where is my crow? Surely he came in with you, Toto?"

"He did," said Toto, "but he hopped off the moment we entered. Did n't like the looks of the visitor, I fancy," he added in a low tone.

Search was made, and finally the crow was discovered huddled together, a disconsolate little bunch of black feathers, in the darkest corner of the cave.

"Come, Jim!" cried Toto, who was the first to catch sight of him. "Come out, old fellow! Why are you rumpling and humping yourself up in that absurd fashion?"

"Is he gone?" asked the crow, opening one eye a very little way, and lifting his head a fraction of an inch from the mass of feathers in which it was buried. "Good Toto, kind Toto, is he gone?   I would not be eaten to-day, Toto, if it could be avoided. *Did* you say he was gone?"

"If you mean the hawk," said Toto, "he is *not* gone; and what is more, he is n't going, for your master has asked him to stay the rest of the winter. But cheer up, old boy! he won't hurt you. Bruin has bound him over to keep the peace, and you must come out and make the best of it."

The unhappy crow begged and protested, but all in vain. Toto caught him up, laughing, and carried him to his master, who set him on his knee, and smoothed his rumpled plumage kindly. The hawk, who was highly gratified by the hermit's invitation, put on his most gracious manner, and soon convinced the crow that he meant him no harm.

"A member of the ancient family of Corvus!" he exclaimed. "Contemporaries, and probably friends, of the early Falcons. Let us also be friends, dear sir; and let the names of James Crow and Ger-Falcon go down together to posterity."

But now Bruin and Pigeon Pretty were eager to hear all the home news from the cottage. They listened with breathless interest to Toto's account of the attempted robbery, and of Coon's noble "defence of the castle," as the boy called it. Miss Mary also received her full share of the credit, nor was the kettle excluded from honorable mention. When all was told, Toto proceeded to unpack the basket he had brought, which contained gingerbread, eggs, apples, and a large can of butter-milk marked "For Bruin." Many were the joyous exclamations called forth by this present of good cheer; and it seemed as if the old hermit could not sufficiently express his gratitude to Toto and his good grandmother.

"Oh, don't!" cried the boy, half distressed by the oft-repeated thanks. "If you only knew how we *like* it! It's so jolly, you know. Besides," he added, "I want you to do something for *me* now, Mr. Baldhead, so that will turn the tables. A shower is coming up, and it is early yet, so I need not go home for an hour. So, will you not tell us a story? We are very fond of stories, — Bruin and Pigeon Pretty and I."

"A story! a story!" cried every one, eagerly.

"A story, hey?" said the good hermit, smiling. "With all my heart, dear lad! And what shall the story be about?"

"About fairies!" replied Toto, promptly. "I have not heard a fairy story for a long time."

"So be it!" said the hermit, after a moment's reflection. "When I was a boy like you, Toto, I lived in Ireland, the very home of the fairy-folk; so I know more about them than most people, perhaps, and this is an Irish fairy story that I am going to tell you."

And settling himself comfortably on his moss-pillows, the hermit began the story of —

CHAPTER XIII.

GREEN JACKET.

" ' It 's Green Men, it 's Green Men,
All in the wood together;
And, oh ! we 're feared o' the Green Men
In all the sweet May weather,' —

"ON'Y I 'm *not* feared o' thim mesilf !'" said Eileen, breaking off her song with a little merry laugh. "Would n't I be plazed to meet wan o' thim this day, in the wud ! Sure, it 'ud be the lookiest day o' me loife."

She parted the boughs, and entered the deep wood, where she was to gather faggots for her mother. Holding up her blue apron carefully, the little girl stepped lightly here and there, picking up the dry brown sticks, and talking to herself all the while, — to keep herself company, as she thought.

"Thin I makes a low curchy," she was saying, "loike that wan Mother made to the lord's lady yistherday, and the Green Man he gi'es me a nod, and —

"'What's yer name, me dear?' says he.

"'Eileen Macarthy, yer Honor's Riverence!' says I. — No! I mustn't say 'Riverence,' bekase he's not a priest, ava'. 'Yer Honor's Grace' wud do better.

"'And what wud ye loike for a prisint, Eily?' says he.

"And thin I'd say — lit me see! what wud I have first? Oh, I know! I'd ask him — Och! what's that? A big green grasshopper, caught be his leg in a spider's wib. Wait a bit, poor crathur, oi'll lit ye free agin."

Full of pity for the poor grasshopper, Eily stooped to lift it carefully out of the treacherous net into which it had fallen. But what was her amazement on perceiving that the creature was not a grasshopper, but a tiny man, clad from head to foot in light green, and with a scarlet cap on his head. The little fellow was hopelessly entangled in the net, from which he made desperate efforts to free himself, but the silken strands were quite strong enough to hold him prisoner.

For a moment Eileen stood petrified with amazement, murmuring to herself, " Howly Saint Bridget! what will I do now at all? Sure, I niver thought I'd find wan really in loife!" but the next moment her kindness of heart triumphed over her fear, and stooping once more she very gently took the little man up between her thumb and finger, pulled away the clinging web, and set him respectfully on the top of a large toadstool which stood conveniently near.

The little Green Man shook himself, dusted his jacket with his red cap, and then looked up at Eileen with twinkling eyes.

"Thank ye, my maiden!" he said kindly. "Ye have saved my life, and ye shall not be the worse for it, if ye *did* take me for a grasshopper."

Eily was rather abashed at this, but the little man looked very kind; so she plucked up her courage, and when he asked, " What is yer name, my dear?" ("jist for all the wurrld the way I thought of," she said to herself) answered bravely, with a low courtesy, "Eileen Macarthy, yer Honor's Riverence — Grace, I mane!" and then she added, "They calls me Eily, most times, at home."

"Well, Eily," said the Green Man, "I suppose ye know who I am?"

"A fairy, plaze yer Honor's Grace!" said Eily, with another courtesy. "Sure, I've aften heerd av yer Honor's people, but I niver thought I'd see wan of yez. It's rale plazed I am, sure enough. Manny's the time Docthor O'Shaughnessy's tell't me there was no sich thing as yez; but I niver belaved him, yer Honor!"

"That's right!" said the Green Man, heartily, "that's very right. Never believe a word he says! And now, Eily, alanna, I'm going to do ye a fairy's turn before I go. Ye shall have yer wish of whatever ye like in the world. Take a minute to think about it, and then make up yer mind."

Eily fairly gasped for breath. Her dreams had then come true; she was to have a fairy wish! Could it possibly be true? And what should she wish for? The magic carpet? The goose that laid eggs of gold? The invisible cloak? Eily had all the old fairy-stories at her tongue's end, for her mother told her one every night as she sat at her spinning. Jack and the Beanstalk, the Sleeping Beauty, the Seven Swans, the Elves that stole Barney Maguire, the Brown Witch, and the Widdy Malone's Pig, — she knew them all, and scores of others besides. Her mother always began the stories with, "Wanst upon a time, and a very good time it was;" or, "Long, long ago, whin King O'Toole was young, and the praties grew all ready biled in the ground;" or, "Wan fine time, whin the fairies danced, and not a poor man lived in Ireland." In this way, the fairies seemed always to be thrown far back into a remote past, which had nothing in common with the real work-a-day world in which Eily lived. But now — oh, wonder of wonders! — now, here was a real fairy, alive and active, with as full power of blessing or banning as if the days of King O'Toole had come again, — and what was more, with good-will to grant to Eileen Macarthy whatever in the wide world she might wish for! The child stood quite still, with her hands clasped, thinking harder than she had ever thought in all her life before; and the Green Man sat on the toadstool and watched her, with eyes which twinkled with some amusement, but no malice.

"Take yer time, my dear," he said, "take yer time! Ye'll not meet a Green Man every day, so make the best o' your chance!"

Suddenly Eily's face lighted up with a sudden inspiration. "Och!" she cried, "sure I have it, yer Riverence's Grace — Honor, I shud say! I have it! it's the di'monds and pearrls I'll have, iv ye plaze!"

"Diamonds and pearls?" repeated the fairy, "what diamonds and pearls? There are a great many in the world. You don't want them *all*, surely?"

"Och, no, yer Honor!" said Eily. "Only wan of aich to dhrop out o' me mouth ivery time I shpake, loike the girrl in the sthory, ye know. Whiniver she opened her lips to shpake, a di'mond an' a pearrl o' the richest beauty dhropped from her mouth. That's what I mane, plaze yer Honor's Grace. Och! wud n't it be beautiful, entirely?"

"Humph!" said the fairy, looking rather grave. "Are ye *quite* sure that this is what you wish for most, Eileen? Don't decide hastily, or ye may be sorry for it."

"Sorry!" cried Eileen, "what for wud I be sorry? Sure I'd be richer than the Countess o' Kilmoggen hersilf, let alone the Queen, be the time I'd talked for an hour. An' I *loove* to talk!" she added softly, half to herself.

The Green Man laughed outright at this. "Well, Eily," he said, "ye shall have yer own way. Stoop down to me here!"

Eileen bent down, and he touched her lips three times with the scarlet tassel of his cap. "Slanegher Banegher!" he said. "The charm is worked. Now go home, Eileen Macarthy, and the good wishes of the Green Men go with ye. Ye will have yer own wish fulfilled as soon as ye cross the thresh-old of yer home. But hark ye now!" he added, impressively. "A day may come when ye will wish with all yer heart to have the charm taken away. If that ever happens, come to this same place with a sprig of holly in yer hand. Strike this toadstool three times, and say, 'Slanegher Banegher, Skeen na Lane!' And now good-by to ye!" and clapping his scarlet cap on his head, the little man leaped from the toad-stool, and instantly disappeared from sight among the ferns and mosses.

Eileen stood still for some time, lost in a dream of wonder and delight. Finally rous-ing herself, she gave a long, happy sigh, and hastily filling her apron with sticks, turned her steps homeward.

The sun was sinking low when she came in sight of the little cabin, at the door of which her mother was standing, looking anxiously in every direction.

"Is it yersilf, Eily?" cried the good wo-man in a tone of relief, as she saw the child approaching. "And where have ye been at all? It 's a wild colleen y' are, to be sprankin' about o' this way, and it nearly sundown. Where have ye been, I 'm askin' ye?"

Eily held up her apronful of sticks with a beaming smile, but answered never a word till she stood on the threshold of the cottage. ("Sure I might lose some," she had been saying to herself, "and that 'ud niver do.") But as soon as she had entered the little room which was kitchen, hall, dining-room, and drawing-room for the Macarthy family, she dropped her bundle of faggots, and clasping her hands together, cried, "Och, mother! what do ye think? Sure ye 'll niver belave me whin I till ye —"

Here she suddenly stopped, for hop! pop! two round shining things dropped from her mouth, and rolled away over the floor of the cabin.

"Howly Michael be me guide!" cried Mrs. Macarthy; "phwhat 's that?"

"It 's marvels! [marbles]" shouted little Phelim, jumping up from his seat by the fire and running to pick up the shining objects. "Eily's got her mouf full o' marvels! Hurroo!"

"They are n't marvels!" said Eily, indignantly. "Wait till I till ye, mother asthore! I wint to the forest as ye bade me, to gather shticks, an' — " hop! pop! out flew two more shining things from her mouth and rolled away after the others.

Mrs. Macarthy uttered a piercing shriek, and clapped her hand over Eileen's mouth. "She's bewitched!" she cried. "Me choild's bewitched, an' shpakin' buttons! Och, wirra! wirra! what'll I do at all? Run, Phelim," she added, "an' call yer father. He's in the praty-patch, loikely. An' ye kape shtill!" she said to Eily, who was struggling vainly to free herself from her mother's powerful grasp. "Kape shtill, I'm tillin' ye, an' don't open yer lips! It's savin' yer body an' sowl I may be this minute. Saint Bridget, Saint Michael, an' blissid Saint Patrick!" she ejaculated piously, "save me choild, an' I'll serve ye on me knees the rist o' me days."

Poor Eily! This was a sad beginning of all her glory. She tried desperately to open her mouth, sure that in a moment she could make her mother understand the whole matter. But Honor Macarthy was a stalwart woman, and Eily's slender fingers could not stir the massive hand which was pressed firmly upon her lips.

At this moment her father entered hastily, with Phelim panting behind him.

"Phwhat's the matther, woman?" he asked anxiously. "Here's Phelim clane out o' his head, an' shcramin' about Eily, an' marvels an' buttons, an' I dunno what all. Phwhat ails the choild?" he added in a tone of great alarm, as he saw Eileen in her mother's arms, flushed and disordered, the tears rolling down her cheeks.

"Och, Dinnis!" cried Honor, "it's bewitched she is, — clane bewitched out o' her sinses, an shpakes buttons out av her mouth wid ivery worrd she siz. Och, me choild! me poor, misfortunate choild! Who wud do ye sich an ill turn as this, whin ye niver harmed annybody since the day ye were born?"

"*Buttons!*" said Dennis Macarthy; "what do ye mane by buttons? How can she shpake buttons, I'm askin' ye? Sure, ye're foolish yersilf, Honor, woman! Lit the colleen go, an' she'll till me phwhat 't is all about."

"Och, av ye don't belave me!" cried Honor. "Show thim to yer father, Phelim! Look at two av thim there in the corner,— the dirrty things!"

Phelim took up the two shining objects cautiously in the corner of his pinafore and carried them to his father, who examined them long and carefully. Finally he spoke, but in an altered voice.

"Lit the choild go, Honor," he said. "I want to shpake till her. Do as I bid ye!" he added sternly; and very reluctantly his wife released poor Eily, who stood pale and trembling, eager to explain, and yet afraid to speak for fear of being again forcibly silenced.

"Eileen," said her father, "'t is plain to be seen that these things are not buttons, but jew'ls."

"Jew'ls!" exclaimed Honor, aghast.

"Ay!" said Dennis; "jew'ls, or gims, whichiver ye plaze to call thim. Now, phwhat I want to know is, where did ye get thim?"

"Oh, Father!" cried Eily; "don't look at me that a-way! Sure, I 've done no harrum! I only —" hop! pop! another splendid diamond and another white, glistening pearl fell from her lips; but she hurried on, speaking as quickly as she could: "I wint to the forest to gather shticks, and there I saw a little Grane Man, all the same loike a hoppergrass, caught be his lig in a spidher's wib; and whin I lit him free he gi' me a wish, to have whativer I loiked bist in the wurrld; an' so I wished, an' I sid —" but by this time the pearls and diamonds were hopping like hailstones all over the cabin-floor; and with a look of deep anger and sorrow Dennis Macarthy motioned to his wife to close

Eileen's mouth again, which she eagerly did.

"To think," he said, "as iver a child o' mine shud shtale the Countess's jew'ls, an' thin till me a pack o' lies about thim! Honor, thim is the beads o' the Countess's nickluss that I was tillin' ye about, that I saw on her nick at the ball, whin I carried the washin' oop to the Castle. An' this misfortunate colleen has shwallied 'em."

"Shwallied 'em!" echoed Honor, incredulously. "How wud she shwally 'em, an' have 'em in her mouth all the toime? An' how wud she get thim to shwally, an' the Countess in Dublin these three weeks, an' her jew'ls wid her? Shame an ye, Dinnis Macarthy! to suspict yer poor, diminted choild of shtalin'! It's bewitched she is, I till ye! Look at the face av her this minute!"

Just at that moment the sound of wheels was heard; and Phelim, who was standing at the open door, exclaimed, —

"Father! here's Docthor O'Shaughnessy

dhrivin' past. Will I shtop him? Maybe he wud know." ·

"Ay, shtop him! shtop him, lad!" cried both mother and father in a breath.

Phelim darted out, and soon returned, followed by the doctor, — a tall, thin man with a great hooked nose, on which was perched a pair of green spectacles.

Eileen had never liked Dr. O'Shaughnessy; and now a cold shiver passed over her as he fixed his spectacled eyes on her and listened in silence to the confused accounts which her father and mother poured into his ear.

"Humph!" he said at last. "Bewitched? 't is very loikely. I' ve known many so of late. Let me see the jew'ls, as ye call thim."

The pearls and diamonds were brought, — a whole handful of them, — and poured into the doctor's hand, which closed suddenly over them, while his dull black eyes shot out a quick gleam under the shading spectacles. The next moment, however, he laughed good-humoredly and turned them carelessly over one by one.

"Why, Dinnis," he said, "'t is aisy to see that ye 've not had mich expeerunce o' jew'ls, me bye, or ye 'd not mistake these bits o' glass an' sich fer thim. No! no! there 's no jew'ls here, wheriver the Countess's are. An' these bits o' trash dhrop out o' the choild's mouth, ye till me, ivery toime she shpakes?"

"Ivery toime, yer Anner!" said Honor. "Out they dhrops, an' goes hoppin' an' leppin' about the room, loike they were aloive."

"I see!" said the doctor. "I understand. This is a very sirrious case, Misther Macarthy, — a very sirrious case *indade*, sirr; an' I'll be free to till ye that I know but *wan* way av curin' it."

"Och, whirrasthru!" cried Mrs. Macarthy. "What is it at all, Docthor alanna? Is it a witch has overlooked her, or what is it? Och, me choild! me poor, diminted choild! will I lose ye this-a-way? Ochone! ochone!" and in her grief she loosed her hold of Eileen and clapped her hands to her own face, sobbing aloud. But before the child could open her lips to speak, she found herself seized in another and no less powerful grasp, while another hand covered her mouth, — not warm and firm like her mother's, but cold, bony, and frog-like. Holding her as in a vice, Dr. O'Shaughnessy spoke once more to her parents.

"I'll save her loife," said he, "and mebbe her wits as well, av the thing's poassible. But it's not here I can do ut at all. I'll take the choild home wid me to me house, and Misthress O'Shaughnessy will tind her as if she wuz her own; and thin I will try th' ixpiriment which is the ownly thing on airth can save her."

"Spirimint?" said Honor. "Sure, there's two, three kinds o' mint growin' here in oor own door-yard, but I dunno av there's anny o' that kind. Will ye make a tay av it, Docthor, or is it a poultuss ye'll be puttin' an her, to dhraw out the witchcraft, loike?"

"Whisht, whisht, woman!" said Dennis, impatiently. "Howld yer prate, can't ye, an' the docthor waitin'? Is there no way ye cud cure her, an' lave her at home thin, Docthor? Faith, I'd be loth to lave her go away from uz loike this, let alone the throuble she 'll be to yez!"

"No throuble at all!" said the doctor, briskly. "At laste," he added more gravely, "naw moor thin I'd gladly take for ye an' yer good woman, Dinnis! Come, help me wid the colleen, now. Aisy does it! Now, thin, oop wid ye, Eily!"

And the next moment Eileen found herself in the doctor's narrow gig, wedged tightly between him and the side of the vehicle.

"Ye can sind her bits o' clothes over by Phelim," said Dr. O'Shaughnessy, as he gathered up the reins, apparently in great haste. "I 'll not shtop now. Good-day t' ye, Dinnis! My respicts to ye, Misthress Macarthy. Ye 'll hear av the choild in a day or two!" And whistling to his old pony, they started off at as brisk a trot as the latter could produce on such short notice.

Poor Eileen! Was this the result of the fairy's gift? She sat still, half-paralyzed with grief and terror, for she made no doubt that the hated doctor was going to do something very, very dreadful to her.

Seeing that she made no effort to free herself, or to speak, her captor removed his hand from her mouth; but not until they were well out of sight and hearing of her parents.

"Now, Eileen," he said, not unkindly, "av ye'll be a good colleen, and not shpake a wurrd, I'll lave yer mouth free. But av ye shpake, so much as to say, 'Bliss ye!' I'll tie up yer jaw wid me pock'-handkercher, so as ye can't open ut at all. D' ye hear me, now?"

Eileen nodded silently. She had not the slightest desire to say "Bliss ye!" to Dr. O'Shaughnessy; nor did she care to fill his rusty old gig, or to sprinkle the high road, with diamonds and pearls.

"That's roight!" said the Doctor, "that's a sinsible gyurrl as ye are. See, now, what a foine bit o' sweet-cake Misthress O'Shaughnessy 'ull be givin' ye, whin we git home."

The poor child burst into tears, for the

word 'home' made her realize more fully that she was going every moment farther and farther away from her own home,—from her kind father, her anxious and loving mother, and dear little Phelim. What would Phelim do at night, without her shoulder to curl up on and go to sleep, in the trundle-bed which they had shared ever since he was a tiny baby? Who would light her father's pipe, and sing him the little song he always liked to hear while he smoked it after supper? These, and many other such thoughts, filled Eileen's mind as she sat weeping silently beside the green-spectacled doctor, who cared nothing about her crying, so long as she did not try to speak.

After a drive of some miles, they reached a tall, dark, gloomy-looking house, which was not unlike the doctor himself, with its small greenish window-panes and its gaunt chimneys. Here the pony stopped, and the doctor, lifting Eileen out of the gig, carried her into the house. Mrs. O'Shaughnessy came out of the kitchen, wiping her hands on her apron, and stared in amazement at the burden in her husband's arms.

"Honor Macarthy's Eily!" she exclaimed. "The Saints protict uz! Is she kilt, or what's the matther?"

"Open the door o' the best room!" said the doctor, briefly. "Open it, woman, I'm tillin' ye!" and entering a large bare room, he set Eileen down hastily on a stool, and then drew a long breath and wiped his brow. "I've got ye!" he said. "Safe and sound I've got ye now, glory for ut! And ye'll not lave this room until ye've made me *King av Ireland!*"

Eileen stared at the man, thinking he had gone mad; for his face was red, and his eyes, from which he had snatched the green spectacles, glittered with a strange light. The same idea flashed into his wife's mind, and she crossed herself devoutly, exclaiming, —

"Howly St. Pathrick, he's clane diminted. 'King,' indade! will ye hear um?"

The doctor turned on her sharply. "Diminted?" he said; "ye'll soon see av I'm

diminted.   I till ye I 'll be King av Ireland
before the month's oot.   Shpake, now, Eileen!
Open yer mouth, alanna, and make yer manners to Misthress O'Shaughnessy."

Thus adjured, Eileen dropped a courtesy,
and said, timidly, "Good day t' ye, Ma'm!
I houp ye 're well!"

Hop! pop! down dropped a pearl and a
diamond, and the doctor, pouncing on them,
held them up in triumph before the eyes of
his astonished wife.

"Div ye see that?" he cried.   "That's a
dimind!   There 's no sich in Queen Victory's
crownd this day.   And look a' that!   That's
a pearrl, an' as big as a marrowfat pay.   The
loike of ut 's not in Ireland, I till ye.   Woman, there 's a fortin' in ivery wurrd-this colleen shpakes!   And she 's goin' to shpake,"
he added, grimly, "and to kape an shpakin',
till Michael O'Shaughnessy is rich enough to
buy all Ireland, — ay, and England too, av
he 'd a mind to!"

"But — but," cried Mrs. O'Shaughnessy,
utterly bewildered by her husband's wild

talk, and by the sight of the jewels, "what does it all mane? Has the choild swallied 'em? And won't she die av 'em, av it's that manny in her stumick?"

"Whisht wid yer foolery!" said her husband, contemptuously. "Swallied 'em, indade! The gyurrl has met a Grane Man, that's the truth of ut; and he's gi'n her a wish, and she's got ut, — and now I've got *her*." And he chuckled, and rubbed his bony hands together, while his eyes twinkled with greed.

"A Grane Man! The saints be good to uz!" cried Mrs. O'Shaughnessy. "Sure, ye always till't me there was no sich thing ava'."

"I lied, thin!" shouted the doctor. "I lied, an' that's all there is to say about ut. Do ye think I'm obleeged to shpake the thruth ivery day in the week to an ignor'nt crathur like yersilf? It's worn out I'd be, body and sowl, at that rate. Now, Eileen Macarthy," he continued, turning to his unhappy little prisoner, "ye are to do as I till ye, an' no harrum 'll coom to ye, an' maybe good. Ye are to sit in this room and *talk;* and ye'll kape an talkin' till the room is *full-up!* d'ye hear me, now?"

"Full-up?" exclaimed Eileen, faintly.

"Full-up!" repeated the doctor. "No less 'll satisfy me, and it's the laste ye can do for all the throuble I've taken forr ye. Misthress O'Shaughnessy an' mesilf 'ull take turns sittin' wid ye, so 'at ye'll have some wan to talk to. Ye'll have plinty to ate an' to dhrink, an' that's more than manny people have in Ireland this day. So lit me hear no complainin'."

With this, the worthy man proceeded to give strict injunctions to his wife to keep the child talking, and not to leave her alone for an instant; and finally he departed, shutting the door behind him, and leaving the captive and her jailer alone together.

Mrs. O'Shaughnessy immediately poured forth a flood of questions, to which Eileen replied by telling the whole pitiful story from beginning to end. It was a relief to be able to speak at last, and to rehearse the whole matter to understanding, if not sympathetic, ears. Mrs. O'Shaughnessy listened and looked, looked and listened, with open mouth and staring eyes. With her eyes shut, she would not have believed her ears; but the double evidence was too much for her.

The diamonds and pearls kept on falling, falling, fast and faster. They filled Eileen's lap, they skipped away over the floor, while the doctor's wife pursued them with frantic eagerness. Each diamond was clear and radiant as a drop of dew, each pearl lustrous and perfect; but they gave no pleasure now to the fairy-gifted child. She could only think of the task that lay before her, — to FILL this great, empty room; of the millions and millions, and yet again millions of gems that must fall from her lips before the floor would be covered even a few inches deep; of the weeks and months, — perhaps the years, — that must elapse before she would see her parents and Phelim again. She remembered the words of the fairy: " A day may come when you will wish with all your heart to have the charm removed." And then, like a flash, came the recollection of those other words: "When that day comes, come here to this spot," and do so and so.

In fancy, Eileen was transported again to the pleasant green forest; was looking at the Green Man as he sat on the toadstool, and begging him to take away this fatal gift, which had already, in one day, brought her so much misery. Harshly on her reverie broke in the voice of Mrs. O'Shaughnessy, asking, —

"And has yer father sold his pigs yit?"

She started, and came back to the doleful world of reality. But even as she answered the woman's question, she made in her heart a firm resolve, — somehow or other, *somehow*, she would escape; she would get out of this hateful house, away from these greedy, grasping people; she would manage somehow to find her way to the wood, and then — then for freedom again! Cheered by her own resolution, she answered the woman composedly, and went into a detailed account of the birth, rearing, and selling of the pigs, which so fascinated her auditor that she was surprised, when the recital was over, to find that it was nearly supper-time.

The doctor now entered, and taking his wife's place, began to ply Eily with questions, each one artfully calculated to bring forth the longest possible reply: —

"How is it yer mother is related to the Countess's auld housekeeper, avick; and why is it, that wid sich grand relations she niver got into the castle at all?"

"Phwhat was that I h'ard the other day about the looky bargain yer father — honest man! — made wid the one-eyed peddler from beyant Inniskeen?" and —

"Is it thrue that yer mother makes all her butther out av skim-milk just by making the sign of the cross — God bless it! — over the churn?"

Although she did not like the doctor, Eily did, as she had said to the Green Man, "*loove* to talk;" so she chattered away, explaining and disclaiming, while the diamonds and pearls flew like hail-stones from her lips, and her host and jailer sat watching them with looks of greedy rapture.

Eily paused, fairly out of breath, just as Mrs. O'Shaughnessy entered, bringing her rather scanty supper. There was quite a pile of jewels in her lap and about her feet, while a good many had rolled to a distance; but her heart sank within her as she compared the result of three hours' steady talking with the end to which the rapacious doctor aspired.

She was allowed to eat her supper in peace, but no sooner was it finished than the questioning began again, and it was not until ten o'clock had struck that the exhausted child was allowed to lay her head down on the rude bed which Mrs. O'Shaughnessy had hastily made up for her.

The next day was a weary one for poor Eily. From morning till night she was obliged to talk incessantly, with only a brief space allowed for her meals. The doctor and his wife mounted guard by turns, each asking questions, until to the child's fancy they seemed like nothing but living interrogation points. All day long, no matter what she was talking about, — the potato-crop, or the black hen that the fox stole, or Phelim's measles, — her mind was fixed on one idea, that of escaping from her prison. If only some fortunate chance would call them both out of the room at once! But, alas! that never happened. There was always a pair of greedy eyes fixed on her, and on the now hated jewels which dropped in an endless stream from her lips; always a harsh voice in her ears, rousing her, if she paused for an instant, by new questions as stupid as they were long.

Once, indeed, the child stopped short, and declared that she could not and would not talk any more; but she was speedily shown the end of a birch rod, with the hint that the doctor "would be loth to use the likes av it on Dinnis Macarthy's choild; but her parints had given him charge to dhrive out the witchcraft be hook or be crook; and av a birch rod was n't first cousin to a crook, what was it at all?" and Eily was forced to find her powers of speech again.

By nightfall of this day the room was ankle-deep in pearls and diamonds. A wonderful sight it was, when the moon looked in at the window, and shone on the lustrous and glittering heaps which Mrs. O'Shaughnessy piled up with her broom. The woman was fairly frightened at the sight of so much treasure, and she crossed herself many times as she lay down on the mat beside Eileen's truckle-bed, muttering to herself, " Michael knows bist, I suppose; but sorrow o' me if I can feel as if there was a blissing an it, ava'!"

The third day came, and was already half over, when an urgent summons came for Doctor O'Shaughnessy. One of his richest patrons had fallen from his horse and broken his leg, and the doctor must come on the instant. The doctor grumbled and swore, but there was no help for it; so he departed, after making his wife vow by all the saints in turn, that she would not leave Eileen's side for an instant until he returned.

When Eily heard the rattle of the gig and the sound of the pony's feet, and knew that the most formidable of her jailers was actually *gone*, her heart beat so loud for joy that she feared its throbbing would be heard. Now, at last, a loop-hole seemed to open for her. She had a plan already in her head, and now there was a chance for her to carry it out. But an Irish girl of ten has shrewdness beyond her years, and no gleam of expression appeared in Eileen's face as she spoke to Mrs. O'Shaughnessy, who had been standing by the window to watch her husband's departure, and who now returned to her seat.

"We'll be missin' the docthor this day, ma'm, won't we?" she said. "He's so agrayable, ain't he, now?"

"He is that!" replied Mrs. O'Shaughnessy, with something of a sigh. "He's rale agrayable, Michael is — whin he wants to be," she added. "Yis, I'll miss um more nor common to-day, for 'tis worn out I am intirely wid shlapin so little these two nights past. Sure, I *can't* shlape, wid thim things a-shparklin' an' a-glowerin' at me the way they do; and now I'll not get me nap at all this afthernoon, bein' I must shtay here and kape ye talkin' till the docthor cooms back. Me hid aches, too, mortial bad!"

"Do it, now?" said Eily, soothingly. "Arrah, it's too bad, intirely! Will I till ye a little shtory that me grandmother hed for the hidache?"

"A shtory for the hidache?" said Mrs. O'Shaughnessy. "What do ye mane by that, I'm askin' ye?"

"I dunno roightly how ut is," replied Eily, innocently, "but Granny used to call this shtory a cure for the hidache, and mebbe ye'd find ut so. An' annyhow it 'ud kape me talkin'," she added meekly, "for 't is mortial long."

"Go an wid it, thin!" said Mrs. O'Shaughnessy, settling herself more comfortably in her chair. "I loove a long shtory, to be sure. Go an, avick!"

And Eily began as follows, speaking in a clear, low monotone : —

"Wanst upon a toime there lived an owld, owld woman, an' her name was Moira Magoyle; an' she lived in an owld, owld house, in an owld, owld lane that lid through an owld, owld wood be the side of an owld, owld shthrame that flowed through an owld, owld shthrate av an owld, owld town in an owld, owld county. An' this owld, owld woman, sure enough, she had an owld, owld cat wid a white nose; an' she had an owld, owld dog wid a black tail, an' she had an owld, owld hin wid wan eye, an' she had an owld, owld cock wid wan leg, an' she had — "

Mrs. O'Shaughnessy yawned, and stirred uneasily on her seat. "Seems to me there's moighty little goin' an in this shtory!" she said, taking up her knitting, which she had dropped in her lap. "I'd loike somethin' a bit more loively, I'm thinkin', av I had me ch'ice."

"Jist wait, ma'm!" said Eily, with quiet confidence, "ownly wait till I coom to the parrt about the two robbers an' the keg o' gunpowdther, an' its loively enough ye 'll foind ut. But I must till ut the same way 'at Granny did, else it 'ull do no good, ava. Well, thin, I was sayin' to ye, ma'm, this owld woman (Saint Bridget be good to her!) she had an owld, owld cow, an' she had an owld, owld shape, an' she had an owld, owld kitchen wid an owld, owld cheer an' an owld, owld table, an' an owld, owld panthry wid an owld, owld churn, an' an owld, owld sauce-pan, an' an owld, owld gridiron, an' an owld, owld — "

Mrs. O'Shaughnessy's knitting dropped again, and her head fell forward on her breast. Eileen's voice grew lower and softer, but still she went on, — rising at the same time, and moving quietly, stealthily, towards the door, —

"An' she had an owld, owld kittle, an' she had an owld, owld pot wid an owld, owld kiver; an' she had an owld, owld jug, an' an owld, owld platther, an' an owld, owld tay-pot — "

Eily's hand was on the door, her eyes were fixed on the motionless form of her jailer; her voice went on and on, its soft monotone now accompanied by another sound, — that of a heavy, regular breathing which was fast deepening into a snore.

"An' she had an owld, owld shpoon, an' an owld, owld fork, an' an owld, owld knife, an' an owld, owld cup, an' an owld, owld bowl, an' an owld, owld, owld — "

The door is open! The story is done! Two little feet go speeding down the long passage, across the empty kitchen, out at the back door, and away, away! Wake, Mrs. O'Shaughnessy! wake! the story is done and the bird is flown!

Surely it was the next thing to flying, the way in which Eily sped across the meadows, far from the hated scene of her imprisonment. The bare brown feet seemed scarcely to touch the ground; the brown locks streamed out on the wind; the little blue apron fluttered wild- ly, like a banner of victory. On! on! on! with panting bosom, with parted lips, with many a backward glance to see if any one were following; on went the little maid, over field and fell, through moss and through mire, till at last — oh, happy, blessed sight! — the dark forest rose before her, and she knew that she was saved.

Quite at the other end of the wood lay the spot she was seeking; but she knew the way well, and on she went, but more carefully now, — parting the branches so that she broke no living twig, and treading cautiously lest she should crush the lady fern, which the Green Men love. How beautiful the ferns were, uncurling their silver-green fronds and spreading their slender arms abroad! How sweetly the birds were singing! How pleasant, how kind, how friendly was everything in the sweet green wood!

And here at last was the oak-tree, and at the foot of it there stood the yellow toadstool, looking as if it did not care about anything or anybody, which in truth it did not: Breathless with haste and eagerness, Eileen tapped the toadstool three times with a bit of holly, saying softly, "Slanegher Banegher! Skeen na lane!" And, lo! and, behold! there sat the Green Man, just as if he had been there all the time, fanning himself with his scarlet cap, and looking at her with a comical twinkle in his sharp little eyes.

"Well, Eily," he said, "is it back so soon ye are? Well, well, I'm not surprised! And how do ye like yer gift?"

"Oh, yer Honor's Riverence — Grace, I mane!" cried poor Eily, bursting into tears, "av ye'll plaze to take it away! Sure it's nearly kilt I am along av it, an' no plazure or coomfort in ut at all at all! Take it away, yer Honor, take it away, and I'll bliss ye all me days!" and, with many sobs, she related the experiences of the past three days. As she spoke, diamonds and pearls still fell in showers from her lips, and half-unconsciously she held up her apron to catch them as they fell, so that by the time she had finished her story she had more than a quart of splendid gems, each as big as the biggest kind of pea.

The Green Man smiled, but not unkindly,

at the recital of Eileen's woes. "Faith, it's a hard time ye 've had, my maiden, and no mistake! But now 't is all over. Hold fast the jewels ye have there, for they 're the last ye 'll get." He touched her lips with his cap, and said, "Cabbala ku! the charm is off."

Eily drew a long breath of relief, and the fairy added, —

"The truth is, Eily, the times are past for fairy gifts of this kind. Few people believe in the Green Men now at all, and fewer still ever see them. Why, ye are the first mortal child I 've spoken to for a matter of two hundred years, and I think ye 'll be the last I ever speak to. Fairy gifts are very pretty things in a story, but they 're not convenient at the present time, as ye see for yourself. There 's one thing I 'd like to say to ye, however," he added more seriously; "an' ye 'll take it as a little lesson-like, me dear, before we part. Ye asked me for diamonds and pearls, and I gave them to ye; and now ye 've seen the worth of that kind for yourself. But there 's jewels and jewels in the world, and if ye choose, Eily, ye can still speak pearls and diamonds, and no harm to yourself or anybody."

"How was yer Honor maning?" asked Eily, wondering. "Sure, I don't undershtand yer Honor at all."

"Likely not," said the little man, "but it's now I'm telling ye. Every gentle and loving word ye speak, child, is a pearl; and every kind deed done to them as needs kindness, is a diamond brighter than all those shining stones in your apron. Ye'll grow up a rich woman, Eily, with the treasure ye have there; but it might all as well be frogs and toads, if with it ye have not the loving heart and the helping hand that will make a good woman of ye, and happy folk of yer neighbors. And now good-by, mavourneen, and the blessing of the Green Men go with ye and stay with ye, yer life long!"

"Good-by, yer Honor," cried Eily, gratefully. "The saints reward yer Honor's Grace for all yer kindness to a poor silly colleen like me! But, oh, wan minute, yer Honor!" she cried, as she saw the little man about to put on his cap. " Will Docthor O'Shaughnessy be King av Ireland? Sure it's the wicked king he 'd make, intirely. Don't let him, plaze, yer Honor!"

Green Jacket laughed long and heartily. "Ho! ho! ho!" he cried. "*King*, is it? Nothing less would suit him, sure enough! Have no fears, Eily, alanna! Dr. O'Shaughnessy has come into his kingdom by this time, and I wish him joy of it."

With these words he clapped his scarlet cap on his head, and vanished like the snuff of a candle.

Now, just about this time Dr. Michael O'Shaughnessy was dismounting from his gig at his own back door, after a long and weary drive. He thought little, however, about his bodily fatigue, for his heart was full of joy and triumph, his mind absorbed in dreams of glory. He could not even contain his thoughts, but broke out into words, as he unharnessed the rusty old pony.

"An' whin I coom to the palace, I 'll knock three times wid the knocker; or maybe there 'll be a bell, loike the sheriff's house (bad luck to um!) at Kilmagore. And the gossoon 'll open the dure, and —

" 'Phwhat 's yer arrind ?' says he.

" 'It 's Queen Victory I 'm wantin',' says I. 'An' ye 'll till her King Michael av Ireland is askin' for her,' I says.

"Thin whin Victory hears that, she 'll coom roonnin' down hersilf, to bid me welkim; an' she 'll take me oop to the best room, an' —

" 'Sit down an the throne, King Michael,' says she. 'The other cheers is n't good enough for the loikes of ye,' says she.

" 'Afther ye, ma'm,' says I, moinding me manners.

" 'An' is there annythin' I can du for ye, to-day, King Michael ?' says she, whin we 've sat down an the throne.

"An' I says, loight and aisy loike, all as if I did n't care, ' Nothin' in loife, ma'm, I 'm obleeged to ye, widout ye 'd lind me the loan o' yer Sunday crownd,' says I, 'be way av a patthern,' says I.

"An' says she — "

But at this moment the royal meditations were rudely broken in upon by a wild shriek which resounded from the house. The door was flung violently open, and Mrs. O'Shaughnessy rushed out like a mad woman.

"She's gone!" she cried wildly. "The colleen's gone, an' me niver shtirrin' from her side! Och, wirra, wirra! what'll I do? It must be the witches has taken her clane up chimley."

Dr. O'Shaughnessy stood for a moment transfixed, glaring with speechless rage at the unhappy woman; then rushing suddenly at her, he seized and shook her till her teeth chattered together.

"Ye've been ashlape!" he yelled, beside himself with rage and disappointment. "Ye've fell ashlape, an' laved her shlip out! Sorrow seize ye, ye're always the black bean in me porridge!" Then flinging her from him, he cried, "I don't care! I'll *be* it!

I'll be king wid what's in there now!" and dashed into the house.

He paused before the door of the best room, lately poor Eily's prison, to draw breath and to collect his thoughts. The door was closed, and from within — hark! what was that sound? Something was stirring, surely. Oh, joy! was his wife mistaken? Waking suddenly from her nap, had she failed to see the girl, who had perhaps been sleeping, too? At all events the jewels were there, in shining heaps on the floor, as he had last seen them, with thousands more covering the floor in every direction, — a king's ransom in half a handful of them. He would be king yet, even if the girl were gone. Cautiously he opened the door and looked in, his eyes glistening, his mouth fairly watering at the thought of all the splendor which would meet his glance.

What did Dr. O'Shaughnessy see? Oh, horror! Oh, dismay, terror, anguish! What did he see? Captive was there none, yet the room was not empty. Jewels were there none, yet the floor was covered; covered with living creatures, — toads, snakes, newts, all hideous and unclean reptiles that hop or creep or wriggle. And as the wretched man stared, with open mouth and glaring eye-balls, oh, horror! they were all hopping, creeping, wriggling towards the open door, — towards him! With a yell beside which his wife's had been a whisper, O'Shaughnessy turned and fled; but after him — through the door, down the passage and out of the house — came hopping, creeping, wriggling his myriad pursuers.

Fly, King Michael! stretch your long legs, and run like a hunted hare over hill and dale, over moss and moor. They are close behind you; they are catching at your heels; they come from every side, surrounding you! Fly, King O'Shaughnessy! but you cannot escape. The Green Men are hunting you, if you could but know it, in sport and in revenge; and three times they will chase you round County Kerry, for thrice three days, till at last they suffer you to drop exhausted in a bog, and vanish from your sight.

And Eily? Eily went home with her apron full of pearls and diamonds, to tell her story again, and this time to be believed. And she grew up a good woman and a rich woman; and she married the young Count of Kilmoggan, and spoke diamonds and pearls all her life long, — at least her husband said she did, and he ought to know.

CHAPTER XIV.

"EGGS! eggs!" cried Toto, springing lightly into the barn, and waving a basket round his head. "Mrs. Speckle, Mrs. Spanish, Dame Clucket, where are you all? I want all the fresh eggs you can spare, please! directly-now-this-very-moment!" and the boy tossed his basket up in the air and caught it again, and danced a little dance of pure enjoyment, while he waited for the hens to answer his summons.

Mrs. Speckle and Dame Clucket, who had been having a quiet chat together in the mow, peeped cautiously over the billows of hay, and seeing that Toto was alone, bade him good-morning.

"I don't know about eggs, to-day, Toto!" said Dame Clucket. "I want to set soon, and I cannot be giving you eggs every day."

"Oh, but I have n't had any for two or three days!" cried Toto. "And I *must* have some to-day. Good old Clucket, dear old Cluckety, give me some, please!"

"Well, I never can refuse that boy, somehow!" said Dame Clucket, half to herself; and Mrs. Speckle agreed with her that it could not be done.

Indeed, it would have been hard to say "No!" to Toto at that moment, for he certainly was very pleasant to look at. The dusty sunbeams came slanting through the high windows, and fell on his curly head, his ruddy-brown cheeks, and honest gray eyes; and as the eyes danced, and the curls danced, and the whole boy danced with the dancing sunbeams, why, what could two soft-hearted old hens do but meekly lead the way to where their cherished eggs lay, warm and white, in their fragrant nests of hay?

"And what is to be done with them?" asked Mrs. Speckle, as the last egg disappeared into the basket.

"Why, don't you know?" cried the boy. "We are going to have a party to-night, — a real party! Mr. Baldhead is coming, and Jim Crow, and Ger-Falcon. And Granny and Bruin are making all sorts of good things, — I'll bring you out some, if I can, dear old Speckly, — and these eggs are for a custard, don't you see?"

"I see!" said Mrs. Speckle, rather ruefully.

"And Coon and I are decorating the kitchen," continued he; "and Cracker is cracking the nuts and polishing the apples; and Pigeon Pretty and Miss Mary are dusting the ornaments, — so you see we are all very busy indeed. Ho! ho! what fun it will be! Good-by, Mrs. Speckle! good-by, Cluckety!" and off ran boy Toto, with his basket of eggs, leaving the two old hens to scratch about in the hay, clucking rather sadly over the memories of their own chickenhood, when they, too, went to parties, instead of laying eggs for other people's festivities.

In the cottage, what a bustle was going on! The grandmother was at her pastry-board, rolling out paste, measuring and filling and covering, as quickly and deftly as if she had had two pairs of eyes instead of none at all. The bear, enveloped in a huge blue-checked apron, sat with a large mortar between his knees, pounding away at something as if his life depended on it. On the hearth sat the squirrel, cracking nuts and piling them up in pretty blue china dishes; and the two birds were carefully brushing and dusting, each with a pair of dusters which she always carried about with her, — one pair gray, and the other soft brown. As for Toto and the raccoon, they were here, there, and everywhere, all in a moment.

"Now, then, where are those greens?" called the boy, when he had carefully deposited his basket of eggs in the pantry.

"Here they are!" replied Coon, appearing at the same moment from the shed, dragging a mass of ground-pine, fragrant fir-boughs, and alder-twigs with their bright coral-red berries. "We will stand these big boughs in the corners, Toto. The creeping stuff will go

over the looking-glass and round the windows. Eh, what do you think?"

"Yes, that will do very well," said Toto.
"We shall need steps, though, to reach so
high, and the step-ladder is broken."

"Never mind!" said Coon. "Bruin will
be the step-ladder. Stand up here, Bruin,
and make yourself useful."

The good bear meekly obeyed, and the raccoon, mounting nimbly upon his shoulders,
proceeded to arrange the trailing creepers
with much grace and dexterity.

"This reminds me of some of our honey-
hunts, old fellow!" he said, talking as he
worked. "Do you remember the famous
one we had in the autumn, a little while
before we came here?"

"To be sure I do!" replied the bear.
"That was, indeed, a famous hunt! It
gave us our whole winter's supply of honey. And we might have got twice as
much more, if it hadn't been for the
accident."

"Tell us about it," said Toto. "I wasn't

with you, you know; and then came the moving, and I forgot to ask you."

"Well, it was a funny time!" said the bear. "Ho! ho! it was a funny time! Coon, you see, had discovered this hive in a big oak-tree, hollow from crotch to ground. He could n't get at it alone, for the clever bees had made it some way down inside the trunk, and he could n't reach far enough down unless some one held him on the outside. So we went together, and I stood on my hind tip-toes, and then he climbed up and stood on my head, and I held his feet while he reached down into the hole."

"Dear me!" said the grandmother, "that was very dangerous, Bruin. I wonder you allowed it."

"Well, you see, dear Madam," replied the bear, apologetically, "it was really the only way. I could n't stand on Coon's head and have him hold *my* feet, you know; and we could n't give up the honey, the finest crop of the season. So —"

"Oh, it was all right!" broke in the raccoon.   "At least, it was at first.   There was such a quantity of honey, — pots and pots of it! — and all of the very best quality.   I took out comb after comb, laying them in the crotch of the tree for safe-keeping till I was ready to go down."

"But where were the bees all the time?" asked Toto.

"Oh, they were there!" replied the raccoon, "buzzing about and making a fine fuss.   They tried to sting me, of course, but my fur was too much for them.   The only part I feared for was my nose, and that I had covered with two or three thicknesses of mullein-leaves, tied on with stout grass.   But as ill-luck would have it, they found out Bruin, and began to buzz about him, too.   One flew into his eye, and he let my feet go for an instant, — just for the very instant when I was leaning down as far as I could possibly stretch to reach a particularly fine comb.   Up went my heels, of course, and down went I."

"Oh, oh!" cried the grandmother.   "My *dear* Coon! do you mean —"

"I mean *down*, dear Madam!" repeated the raccoon, gravely, — "the very downest down there was, I assure you. I fell through that hollow tree as the falling star darts through the ambient heavens. Luckily there was a soft bed of moss and rotten wood at the bottom, or I might not have had the happiness of being here at this moment. As it was —"

"As it was," interrupted the bear, "I dragged him out by the tail through the hole at the bottom. Ho! ho! I wish you could have seen him. He had brought the whole hive with him. Indeed, he looked like a hive himself, covered from head to foot with wax and honey, and a cloud of bees buzzing about him. But he had a huge piece of comb in each paw, and was gobbling away, eating honey, wax, bees and all, as if nothing had happened."

"Naturally," said the raccoon, "I am of a saving disposition, as you know, and cannot bear to see anything wasted. It is not generally known that bees add a slight pungent flavor to the honey, which is very agreeable.

Ve-ry agreeable!" he repeated, throwing his head back, and screwing up one eye, to contemplate the arrangement he had just completed. "How is that, Toto; pretty, eh?"

"Very pretty!" said Toto. "But, see here, if you keep Bruin there all day, we shall never get through all we have to do. Jump down, that's a good fellow, and help me to polish these tankards."

When all was ready, as in due time it was, surely it would have been hard to find a pleasanter looking place than that kitchen. The clean white walls were hung with wreaths and garlands, while the great fir-boughs in the corners filled the air with their warm, spicy fragrance. Every bit of metal — brass, copper, or steel — was polished so that it shone resplendent, giving back the joyous blaze of the crackling fire in a hundred tiny reflections. The kettle was especially glorious, and felt the importance of its position keenly.

"I trust you have no unpleasant feeling about this," it said to the black soup-kettle.

"Every one cannot be beautiful, you know. If you are useful, you should be content with that."

"Hubble ! bubble ! Bubble ! hubble !
Some have the fun, and some have the trouble !"

replied the soup-kettle. "My business is to make soup, and I make it. That is all I have to say."

The table was covered with a snowy cloth, and set with glistening crockery — white and blue — and clean shining pewter. The great tankard had been brought out of its cupboard, and polished within an inch of its life ; while the three blue ginger-jars, filled with scarlet alder-berries, looked down complacently from their station on the mantelpiece. As for the floor, I cannot give you an idea of the cleanness of it. When everything else was ready and in place, the bear had fastened a home-made scrubbing-brush to each of his four feet, and then executed a sort of furious scrubbing-dance, which fairly made the house shake ; and the result was a shining purity which vied with that of the linen table-cloth, or the very kettle itself.

And you should have seen the good bear, when his toilet was completed! The scrubbing-brushes had been applied to his own shaggy coat as well as to the floor, and it shone, in its own way, with as much lustre as anything else; and in his left ear was stuck a red rose, from the monthly rose-bush which stood in the sunniest window and blossomed all winter long. It is extremely uncomfortable to have a rose stuck in one's ear, — you may try it yourself, and see how you like it; but Toto had stuck it there, and nothing would have induced Bruin to remove it. And you should have seen our Toto himself, carrying his own roses on his cheeks, and enough sunshine in his eyes to make a thunder-cloud laugh! And you should have seen the great Coon, glorious in scarlet neck-ribbon, and behind his ear (*not* in it! Coon was not Bruin) a scarlet feather, the gift of Miss Mary, and very precious. And you should have seen the little squirrel, attired in his own bushy

tail, and rightly thinking that he needed no
other adornment; and the parrot and the
wood-pigeon, both trim and elegant, with
their plumage arranged to the last point of
perfection. Last of all, you should have seen
the dear old grandmother, the beloved Madam, with her snowy curls and cap and kerchief; and the ebony stick which generally
lived in a drawer and silver paper, and only
came out on great occasions. How proud
Toto was of his Granny! and how the others
all stood around her, gazing with wondering
admiration at her gold-bowed spectacles (for
those she usually wore were of horn) and the
large breastpin, with a weeping-willow displayed upon it, which fastened her kerchief.

"Made out of your grandfather's tail, did
you say, Toto?" said the bear, in an undertone. "Astonishing!"

"No, no, Bruin!" cried the boy, half pet-
tishly. "Made out of his *hair!* Surely you
might know by this time that we have no
tails."

"True! true!" murmured the bear, apologetically. "I beg your pardon, Toto, boy. You are not really vexed with old Bruin?"

Toto rubbed his curly head affectionately against the shaggy black one, in token of amity, and the bear continued : —

" When Madam was a young grandmother, was she as beautiful as she is now?"

" Why, yes, I fancy so," replied Toto. " Only she was n't a grandmother then, you know."

" How so?" inquired Bruin. " What else could she be? You never were anything but a boy, were you?"

" Oh, no, of course not!" said Toto. "But that is different. When Granny was young, she was a girl, you see."

" I don't believe it!" said the bear, stoutly. " I — do — *not* — believe it! I saw a girl once — many years ago; it squinted, and its hair was frowzy, and it wore a hideous basket of flowers on its head, — a dreadful creature! Madam never can have looked like *that!*"

At this moment a knock was heard at the door.   Toto flew to open it, and with a beaming face ushered in the old hermit, who entered leaning on his stick, with his crow perched on one shoulder and the hawk on the other.

Then, what greetings followed! What introductions! What bows and courtesies, and whisking of tails and flapping of wings! The hermit's bow in greeting to the old lady was so stately that Master Coon was consumed with a desire to imitate it; and in so doing, he stepped back against the nose of the tea-kettle and burned himself, which caused him to retire suddenly under the table with a smothered shriek. (But the kettle was glad.) And the hawk and the pigeon, the raccoon and the crow, the hermit and the bear, all shook paws and claws, and vowed that they were delighted to see each other; and what is more, they really *were* delighted, which is not always the case when such vows are made.

Now, when all had become well acquainted, and every heart was prepared to be merry, they sat down to supper; and the supper was not one which was likely to make them less cheerful. For there was chicken and ham, and, oh, such a mutton-pie! You never saw such a pie; the standing crust was six inches high, and solid as a castle wall; and on that lay the upper-crust, as lightly as a butterfly resting on a leaf; while inside was store of good mutton, and moreover golden eggballs and tender little onions, and gravy as rich as all the kings of the earth put together. Ay! and besides all that there was white bread like snow, and brown bread as sweet as clover-blossoms, and jam and gingerbread, and apples and nuts, and pitchers of cream and jugs of buttermilk. Truly, it does one's heart good to think of such a supper, and I only wish that you and I had been there to help eat it. However, there was no lack of hungry mouths, with right good-will to keep their jaws at work, and for a time there was little conversation around the table, but much joy and comfort in the good victuals.

The good grandmother ate little herself, though she listened with pleasure to the stirring sound of knives and forks, which told her that her guests were well and pleasantly employed. Presently the hermit addressed her, and said : —

"Honored Madam, you will be glad to know that there has been a great change in the weather during the past week. Truly, I think the spring is at hand; for the snow is fast melting away, the sun shines with more than winter's heat, and the air to-day is mild and soft."

At these words there was a subdued but evident excitement among the company. The raccoon and the squirrel exchanged swift and significant glances; the birds, as if by one unconscious impulse, ruffled their feathers and plumed themselves a little. But boy Toto's face fell, and he looked at the bear, who, for his part, scratched his nose and looked intently at the pattern on his plate.

"It has been a long, an unusually long, season," continued the hermit, "though doubtless it has seemed much shorter to you in your cosey cottage than to me in my lonely cavern. But I have lived the forest-life long enough to know that some of you, my friends," and he turned with a smile to the forest-friends, "must be already longing to hear the first murmur of the greenwood spring, and to note in tree and shrub the first signs of awakening life."

There was a moment of silence, during which the raccoon shifted uneasily on his seat, and looked about him with restless, gleaming eyes. Suddenly the silence was broken by a singular noise, which made every one start. It was a long-drawn sound, something between a snort, a squeal, and a snore; and it came from — where *did* it come from?

"Was it you?" said one.

"No! was it you?"

"It seemed to come," said the hawk, who sat facing the fire, "from the wall near the fireplace."

At this moment the sound was heard again, louder and more distinct, and this time it certainly *did* come from the wall, — or rather from the cupboard in the wall, near the fireplace.

"Yaw-haw! yaw-ah-hee!" Then came a muffled, scuffling sound, and finally a shrill peevish voice cried, "Let me out! let me out, I say! Coon, I know your tricks; let me out, or I'll tell Bruin this minute!"

The bear burst into a volcanic roar of laughter, which made the hermit start and turn pale in spite of himself, and going to the cupboard he drew out the unhappy woodchuck, hopelessly entangled in his worsted covering, from which• he had been vainly struggling to free himself.

Oh, how they all laughed! It seemed as they would never have done laughing; while every moment the woodchuck grew more furious, — squeaking and barking, and even trying to bite the mighty paw which held him. But the wood-pigeon had pity on him, and with a few sharp pulls broke the worsted net, and begged Bruin to set him down on the table. This being done, Master Chucky found his nose within precisely half an inch of a most excellent piece of dried beef, upon which he fell without more ado, and stayed not to draw breath till the plate was polished clean and dry.

That made every one laugh again, and altogether they were very merry, and fell to playing games and telling stories, leaving the woodchuck to try the keen edge of his appetite upon every dish on the table. By-and-by, however, this gentleman could eat no more; so he wiped his paws and whiskers, brushed his coat a little, and then joined in the sport with right good-will.

It was a pleasant sight to see the great bear blindfolded, chasing Toto and Coon from one corner to another, in a grand game of blindman's buff; it was pleasant to see them playing leap-frog, and spin-the-platter, and many a good old-fashioned game besides. Then, when these sat down to rest and recover their breath, what a treat it was to see the four birds dance a quadrille, to the music of Toto's fiddle! How they fluttered and sidled, and hopped and bridled! How gracefully Miss Mary courtesied to the stately hawk; and how jealous the crow was of this rival, who stood on one leg with such a perfect grace!

Ah! altogether that was a party worth going to. And when late in the evening it broke up, and the visitors started on their homeward walk, all declared it was the merriest time they had yet had together, and all wished that they might have many more such times. And yet each one knew in his heart, — and grieved to know, — that it was the last, and that the end was come.

CHAPTER XV.

YES, the end was come! The woodchuck sounded, the next morning, the note which had for days been vibrating in the hearts of all the wild creatures, but which they had been loth to strike, for Toto's sake.

"Come!" he said. "It is time we were off. I don't know what you are all thinking of, to stay on here after you are awake. I smelt the wet earth and the water, and the sap running in the trees, even in that dungeon where you had put me. The young reeds will soon be starting beside the pool, and it is my work to trim them and thin them out properly; besides, I am going to dig a new burrow, this year. I tell you I must be off."

And the squirrel with a chuckle, and the wood-pigeon with a sigh, and the raccoon

with a strange feeling which he hardly under-
stood, but which was not all pleasure, echoed
the words, "We must be off!" Only the
bear said nothing, for he was in the wood-
shed, splitting kindling-wood with a fury of
energy which sent the chips flying as if he
were a saw-mill.

So it came to pass that on a soft, bright
day in April, when the sun was shining
sweetly, and the wind blew warm from the
south, and the buds were swelling on willow
and alder, the party of friends stood around
the door of the little cottage, exchanging
farewells, half merry, half sad, and wholly
loving.

"After all, it is hardly good-by!" said
the squirrel, gayly. "We shall be here half
the time, just as we were last summer; and
the other half, Toto will be in the forest. Eh,
Bruin?"

But Bruin rubbed his nose with his right
paw, and said nothing.

"And you will come to the forest, too,
dear Madam!" cried the raccoon, "will

you not? You will bring the knitting and the gingerbread, and we will have picnics by the pool, and you will learn to love the forest as much as Toto does. Won't she, Bruin?"

But Bruin rubbed his nose with his left paw, and still said nothing.

"And when my nest is made, and my little ones are fledged," cooed the wood-pigeon in her tender voice, " their first flight shall be to you, dear Madam, and their first song shall tell you that they love you, and that we love you, every day and all day. For we do love you; don't we, Bruin?"

But the bear only looked helplessly around him, and scratched his head, and again said nothing.

"Well," said Toto, cheerily, though with a suspicion of a quiver in his voice, " you are all jolly good fellows, and we have had a merry winter together. Of course we shall miss you sadly, Granny and I; but as you say, Cracker, we shall all see each other every day; and I am longing for the forest, too, almost as much as you are."

"Dear friends," said the blind grandmother, folding her hands upon her stick, and turning her kindly face from one to the other of the group, — "dear friends, merry and helpful companions, this has indeed been a happy season that we have spent together. You have, one and all, been a comfort and a help to me, and I think you have not been discontented yourselves; still, the confinement has of course been strange to you, and we cannot wonder that you pine for your free, wildwood life. Coon, give me your paw! it is a mischievous paw, but it has never played any tricks on me, and has helped me many and many a time. My little Cracker, I shall miss your merry chatter as I sit at my spinning-wheel. Mary, and Pigeon Pretty, let me stroke your soft feathers once more, by way of 'good-by.' Woodchuck, I have seen little of you, but I trust you have enjoyed your visit, in your own way.

"And now, last of all, Bruin! my good, faithful Bruin! come here and let me shake your honest, shaggy paw, and thank you for all that you have done for me and for my boy." She paused, but no answer came.

"Why, where *is* Bruin?" cried Toto, starting and looking round; "surely he was here a minute ago. Bruin! Bruin! where are you?"

But no deep voice was heard, roaring cheerfully, "Here, Toto boy!" No shaggy form came in sight. Bruin was gone.

"He has gone on ahead, probably," said the raccoon; "he said something, this morning, about not liking to say good-by. Come, you others, we must follow our leader. Good-by, dear Madam! See you to-morrow, Toto!"

"Good-by!"

"Good-by!"

"Good-by!" cried all the others.

And with many a backward glance, and many a wave of paw, or tail, or fluttering wing, the party of friends took their way to the forest home.

Boy Toto stood with his hands in his pockets, looking after them with bright, wide-open eyes. He did not cry, — it was a part of Toto's creed that boys did not cry after they had left off petticoats, — but he felt that if he had been a girl, the tears might have come in spite of him. So he stared very hard, and puckered his mouth in a silent whistle, and felt of the marbles in his pockets, — for that is always a soothing and comforting thing to do.

"Toto, dear," said his grandmother, "do you think our Bruin is really *gone*, without saying a word of farewell to us?"

"So it seems!" said the boy, briefly.

"I am very much grieved!" cried the old lady, putting her handkerchief to her sightless eyes, — "very, very much grieved! If it had been Coon, now, I should not have been so much surprised; but for Bruin, our faithful friend and helper, to leave us so, seems —"

"*Hello!*" cried Toto, starting suddenly, "what is that noise?"

Both listened, and, lo! on the quiet air came the sharp crashing sound of an axe.

"He's there!" cried the boy. "He *isn't* gone! I'll go —" and with that he went, as if he had been shot out of a catapult.

Rushing into the wood-shed, he caught sight of the well-beloved shaggy figure, just raising the axe to deliver a fearful blow at an unoffending log of wood. Flinging his arms round it (the figure, not the axe nor the log), he gave it such a violent hug that bear and boy sat down suddenly on the ground, while the axe flew to the other end of the shed.

"Oh, Bruin, Bruin!" cried Toto, "we thought you were gone, without saying a word to us. How could you frighten us so?"

The bear rubbed his nose confusedly, and muttered something about "a few more sticks in case of cold weather."

But here Toto burst out laughing in spite of himself, for the shed was piled so high with kindling-wood that the bear sat as it were at the bottom of a pit whose sides of neatly split sticks rose high above his head.

"You old goose!" cried the boy. "There's kindling-wood enough here to last us ten years, at the very least. Come away! Granny wants you. She thought—"

"There will be more butter to make, now, Toto, since that new calf has come," said the bear, breaking in with apparent irrelevance.

"I suppose there will!" said the boy, staring. "What of it?"

"And that pig is getting too big for you to manage," continued Bruin, in a serious tone. "He was impudent to *me* the other day, and I had to take him up by the tail and swing him, before he would apologize. Now, you *couldn't* take him up by the tail, Toto, much less swing him, and there is no use in your deceiving yourself about it."

"Of course I couldn't!" cried Toto. "No one could, except you, old monster. But what *are* you thinking about that for, now? Come along, I tell you! Granny will think you are gone, after all." And catching the bear by the ear, he led him back in triumph to the cottage-door, crying, "Granny, Granny! here he is! Now give him a good scolding, please, for frightening us so."

But the grandmother never scolded. She only stroked the shaggy black fur, and said,

"Bruin, dear! my good, faithful, true-hearted Bruin! I could not bear to think that you had left me without saying good-by. That hurt me very much. But you would not have done it, would you, Bruin? We ought to have known you better."

The bear looked about him distractedly, and bit his paw severely, as if to relieve his feelings. "Yes I would!" he cried. "At least, if I meant to say good-by. I would n't say it, because I could n't. But I don't mean to say it, — I mean I don't mean to do it. If you don't want me in the house, — being large and clumsy, as I am well aware, and ugly too, — I can sleep out by the pump, and come in to do the work. But I cannot leave the boy, please, dear Madam, nor you. And the calf wants attention, and that pig *ought* to be swung at least once a week, and — and — "

But there was no need of further speech, for Toto's arms were clinging round his neck, and Toto's voice was shouting exclamations of delight; and the grandmother was shaking his great black paw, and calling him her best friend, her dearest old Bruin, and telling him that he should never leave them.

And, in fact, he never did leave them. He settled down quietly in the little cottage, and washed and churned, baked and brewed, milked the cow and kept the pig in order. Happy was the good bear, and happy was Toto, in those pleasant days. For every afternoon, when the work was done, they welcomed one or all of their forest friends; or else they sought the green, beloved forest themselves, and sat beside the fairy pool, and wandered in the cool green mazes where all was sweetness and peace, with rustle of leaves and murmur of water, and chirp of bird and insect. But evening found them always at the cottage door again, bringing their woodland joyousness to the blind grandmother, making the kitchen ring with laughter as they related the last exploits of the raccoon or the squirrel, or described the courtship of the parrot and the crow.

And if you had asked any of the three, as

they sat together in the porch, who was the happiest person in the world, why, Toto and the Grandmother would each have answered, "I!" But Bruin, who had never studied grammar, and knew nothing whatever about his nominatives and his accusatives, would have roared with a thunder-burst of enthusiasm,

"ME !!!"

University Press: John Wilson & Son, Cambridge.